# TENDER TRAP

# TENDER TRAP

Gillian Kaye

Chivers Press  •  G.K. Hall & Co.
Bath, England     Thorndike, Maine USA

This Large Print edition is published by Chivers Press, England, and by G.K. Hall & Co., USA.

Published in 2000 in the U.K. by arrangement with Robert Hale Ltd.

Published in 2000 in the U.S. by arrangement with Robert Hale Ltd.

U.K. Hardcover   ISBN 0-7540-3931-5   (Chivers Large Print)
U.K. Softcover    ISBN 0-7540-3932-3   (Camden Large Print)
U.S. Softcover    ISBN 0-7838-8763-9   (Nightingale Series Edition)

The text of this Large Print edition is unabridged.
Other aspects of the book may vary from the original edition.

Set in 16 pt. New Times Roman.

Printed in Great Britain on acid-free paper.

**British Library Cataloguing in Publication Data available**

**Library of Congress Cataloging-in-Publication Data**

Kaye, Gillian.
        Tender trap / Gillian Kaye.
            p.      cm.
        ISBN 0-7838-8763-9 (lg. print : sc : alk. paper)
        1. Large type books.    I. Title.
        [PR6061.A943T46      2000]
        823'.914—dc21                                                99–41970

# CHAPTER ONE

Helen stood at the window of her flat looking at the rooftops of London in the cold dreary sleet of a day in early January. London, the city of her dreams; she had come so full of them, but the metropolis had become the London of her shattered hopes. All she could see as she stood there were the wet slates of the houses opposite and row after row of smoke-begrimed chimneys, pots blackened with smoke long past and no longer the symbol of the flickering, warm flames of a coal fire which brought comfort to its inhabitants. The scene out of the window reflected her mood, depressed, bleak, nowhere a green leaf or a blade of grass, not even a patterned branch of a bare tree against the grey sky.

She was an attractive girl. She wore her long, brown hair loose and it curled softly at the ends just below her shoulders; her face was small and her large grey eyes were her loveliest feature; her finely shaped mouth was often set in a serious mood, but a cheerful word would make her smile easily, a smile that lit up her face and eyes. Small-boned, she was no more than five feet three inches high, but her whole slim body was beautifully proportioned. She took a great deal of care in choosing her clothes and always looked well-groomed, but at the bottom of her heart she was happier in more casual country wear, liking nothing better than to go off for a long walk in denims and open-necked shirt, something she had not been able to do since she had come to work in London.

She had moved to the city almost three years ago from her country home in a small Dorset village, where she lived with her parents and her elder sister. When she left school she worked in an office in Dorchester, but there was no future in it and her parents persuaded her to have a year off and take a secretarial course. The friends she had made on the course were eager to work in London, and Helen was soon caught up in their enthusiasm. It had been an exciting time, finding a flat and settling in to her job as a receptionist at Sadlers, a large estate agents. Even more exciting was meeting Jeremy and falling in love—but all that was over now.

'Are you still brooding about him?' Helen turned from the window as her flat-mate Jenny called to her across the room. Her mind which had been blank with the winter London gloom as she stared out of the window, was suddenly filled with a rush of emotion at Jenny's words. Him. Jeremy. She pictured his dark hair and smiling good looks, his companionship of many months, his constant wish to be with her, his love. She had thought it was love. So sure was she of her love for him, her desire always to be near him, her dreams of a future never apart from him. His kisses and his love-making, his soft tender words had never left her in any doubt that his feelings were the same as hers. Oh Jeremy, Jeremy . . .

'He was only after one thing.' It was Jenny again, cutting across her train of thought. 'He was so sure of your giving in to him. Once he knew it was wedding bells that were ringing in your head, it was all over.'

Helen knew that Jenny was forcing her to see the situation in its true light. Jenny, down to earth, practical Jenny, had never liked Jeremy, regarding him as a good-for-nothing charmer. But she had never been able to make Helen see him as he really was. They say that love is blind, thought Helen, and only now am I beginning to open my eyes.

She had been happy and settled at Sadlers. As receptionist she was meeting people all day long and she enjoyed typing out the details of the houses and flats for sale. It had been into this happy office that Jeremy Westcott had walked in as a new surveyor, last summer. He was immediately popular and Helen watched him from her desk, with secret, almost unrecognised longings that he might turn and notice her. When he stayed behind after they had closed one evening to talk to her, and then the following day asked her to go out to dinner with him, she felt a tumult of emotions she could not describe even to herself. Joy, excitement, nervousness, but also a deep sense that this was right. Day after day, she was whirled deeper and deeper into love; she was happy, content, so sure that this was the love she had always known would one day come to her. She was remembering now, with anguish in her heart, the visits to the theatre, the dinner dates, and above all the trips out of London on fine summer evenings. Her kaleidoscope of thoughts stopped as one picture became clear and vivid, a memorable evening but one which sowed the first seeds of doubt. She knew that Jeremy loved her, he said so on every occasion they met, he said so with deep ardent kisses which she returned, her body telling her that this indeed was a wonderful love.

The memory of that evening was with her still, sharply etched in her mind. The drive out of London to Henley, the boat taking them slowly up the river, Jeremy strongly pulling the oars and laughing at her for her idle enjoyment. They pulled up the boat by the sloping willows, long slender leaves gently moving in the breeze. Leaving the boat and walking along the bank, they sat and watched the late sun turning the water into streams of glittering silver—a paradise of soft greens and quiet sounds broken only by the murmur of their voices. Jeremy's lips were soft on her throat; quivering at his touch she moved her mouth to meet his. Feeling the strength of his desire, his hand on her breast caressing and persuasive, then moving gently to the soft flesh on the inside of her thigh, arousing shivers of longing, her throbbing body suddenly stiffened. Before she knew what was happening she had torn herself from his grasp and had tripped and sobbed and stumbled back to the boat. A furiously angry Jeremy followed but she could only sob and tremble, words would not come to explain her chaotic thoughts and emotions. She could not understand them even deep within herself, the love she felt for him but did not feel ready to express in its fullest meaning.

For weeks after that she saw him only in the office, and went through an agony of self-doubt, tortured by having to see him, longing to be near him once again. He was pleasant to her but distant and she thought she had lost him forever. Then as the autumn came, little things brought them back together: one day they shared lunch; another time she went out with him to view a house, there was a sudden rainstorm and he took her home. Once more love blossomed and this time she felt more sure; happy that her love was truly returned, she had inward visions and feelings of a future together . . .

Future together—it was as though a shutter had snapped over her mind, she pressed her forehead to the window and tried not to relive the horror of her realization of what she had

5

seen; Jeremy in the car with another girl, the questions, the arguments, the terrible row they had had. He had called her dreadful names which she had tried to forget, because she would not give her whole self to him. She knew she loved him and wanted his love but something always held her back. Finally she knew she had lost him and that the words that Jeremy had spoken were right.

She faltered and went over to Jenny who had been regarding her with some concern. 'I suppose I was fool enough to believe that he wanted marriage just as I did. I never believed what you said about him. I loved him—too much. Now it's finished. How am I going to be able to go back to work and face him? I can't. I can't. I hate him. I hate Sadlers. I hate London. I'd do anything to get away from this gloomy view of roofs and chimneys, the noise and the traffic . . .'

Sensible as always, Jenny interrupted her: 'But you've got to face up to him! Don't let him see what he has done to you. Sadlers is a marvellous place to work and you've got a good job. You've always liked it there ever since you came to London.'

'Well I don't like it any longer. I don't know why I left Dorset. At least there was clean fresh air there, not these horrible city fumes.'

'But, Helen, you can't go back there, back to your parents. I know they'd love to have you but it's running away, taking a step back.'

'You're making me face up to things aren't you? You've made me think about it.' Helen sounded a shade more positive. 'I'll look for another job, somewhere in the country, as far away from here and Jeremy as possible.'

'But you can't leave the flat!' The two girls had been good friends and had shared for over two years. 'You've always loved having a flat in London, near the theatres and the West End.'

Helen's mood was changing with every word. 'Yes I can. I'm sorry, Jenny, I shall hate to leave you, but you've opened my eyes at last. London has its attractions, but it's not where I want to be. Where's that copy of *The Lady*? I'm going to look for something straight away.'

Jenny groaned, half in despair, but willing to humour her friend. 'You've changed all of a sudden. It must be the weather. It's been a rotten January and it's a depressing month at the best of times.'

Helen was reading out of the magazine. 'Secretary and companion to an author in Wales.'

'Too far away and too boring; you can't shut yourself right away.'

'Cook/housekeeper to a farmer in Devon. I wouldn't be far from home. No, I can't see myself as a cook, even if it is the great outdoor life. Wait a moment.' Helen paused. 'Listen to this. Receptionist/secretary required for two doctors in small country practice.

7

Accommodation provided. Hexton, where's that?'

'It's in Yorkshire about 30 miles from Leeds. We went through it on our way to the Dales when we had that weekend up there last year . . .'

Helen interrupted her. 'But it was lovely there, all those green fields and grey stone walls, and even from the car you could see how lovely it was on top of the moors. And it's what I'm qualified to do—receptionist and secretary. And I wouldn't have to worry about looking for a flat. I don't suppose the money is as good as London but if you don't have to pay a rent it makes a lot of difference. Shall I try for it?' Helen was enthusiastic and smiled at her friend.

Jenny nodded. 'It sounds quite good if that's what you're sure you'd like. It seems rather off the beaten track to me.'

But Helen had made up her mind. Depressing thoughts of London and her job and above all Jeremy were pushed to the back of her mind. She dragged out the typewriter and soon had an application typed out.

'If I know there's a chance of escape it won't seem so bad going back to work tomorrow,' she said cheerfully. 'You never know, in a month's time I may be two hundred miles away.'

It was in fact two weeks later that the Inter-City train, that had brought her from London,

8

pulled in at Leeds station. Helen recalled the instructions in the letter she had received from Dr Mark Sinclair asking her to go for an interview. She walked slowly to the bus station in a damp drizzle, feeling anxious and nervous, and yet it was with an undercurrent of excitement that she boarded the local bus to Hexton. She knew the bus journey would take her over an hour and she settled in the seat listening to friendly Yorkshire voices chattering and laughing all around her. In all the cheerful noise, somehow she didn't feel strange but enveloped in a reassuring warmth, and as the bus reached the outskirts of Leeds and housing estates changed to fields and trees she began to feel more relaxed. As she looked out of the window she liked the green-grey feel of the countryside; the small villages had an air of permanence. At each stop there was an exchange of passengers, an exchange of greetings. Some got off the bus laden with their city shopping, some got on for shorter journeys home. All spoke to the driver as they entered and Helen could not but help contrast their slow solid friendliness with the silent, anonymous rush of the London passenger.

Her thoughts turned to her destination and Dr Mark Sinclair; the advertisement had mentioned two doctors and in her imagination she had supplied one with an elderly lined face and gruff but kindly manner—she hoped he would be Dr Sinclair and that he would

9

interview her. The second doctor she envisaged as being young, not long from medical school, perhaps just married. She wondered for the hundredth time what the surgery would be like and if that was where she would live if she got the job.

They were now entering the small town; she didn't really remember Hexton and felt a rush of pleasure as the bus pulled up in a broad market-square. The whole place had a solid feeling of history, stone-built houses now turned into small shops, the eighteenth-century façades and graciously proportioned windows blending with the Victorian buildings; there was little more recent than that. The centre of the square was now used as a car park except at one end where the bright awnings of bustling market-stalls could be seen.

Helen got off the bus and made her way to one of the stalls to ask where Bridge Street was, and discovered that the street and the doctors' surgery lay just off the square. She was told to take the road to the right that led down to the river, and as she turned the corner and saw the view that opened up before her, nervousness and apprehension seemed to vanish. The houses of Bridge Street were built in the same style as the shops she had just seen, tall Georgian town houses now mainly used as solicitors' or accountants' offices, and beyond was the old bridge which took the road

10

into the next dale, straddling the River Garth. But what filled her with delight was the sudden rise of the land in the distance, and the farms and fields of the lower slopes with their patchwork of grey stone walls. Above and opening to the sky was the rough moorland, with outcrops of rocks breaking its majestic sweep. Helen caught her breath. She had not expected the open moor to be so near to the town. Her heart lifted as confidence surged through her; she didn't have to take a step further to know that this was where she wanted to be. She was filled with a determination to get the job, to come to this lovely place and to leave the troubles and hurts of London behind her.

She realised she had been standing at the corner for a few minutes and that it was time to be looking for Bridge House which she imagined must be somewhere near the river. She had no difficulty finding it and again the sense of delight gave her a feeling of eager anticipation. It was not quite on the river bank; a row of cottages separated the house from the actual river. Bridge House was a large three-storeyed Georgian building set back from the road by a gravelled drive lined with evergreen shrubs. It was a sober building but in its setting combined with the background of hills it gave a sense of mellowness and solidity which proclaimed two centuries of life and usefulness.

11

At the front door, the shining, polished plaque announced the surgery hours and the names of the doctors: Dr Thomas Wharton; Dr Mark Sinclair. Helen took a deep breath and rang the bell, the door opened and the short white-haired person who stood there was unsmiling; she looked serious, worried, even stressed. Helen hesitated.

'I am Helen Wainwright. I have an interview with Dr Sinclair this afternoon.'

'Come in, come in, don't stand there. I'm sure Doctor is ready, but I'll put you in the waiting room and go and ask him. You come in here and I'll tell him. Though I don't know what kind of reception you're going to get what with Miss Emma running off again. You sit there and I'll come back and tell when he's ready. I'm sure I don't know.'

Helen sat down, bewildered and perplexed by this rush of words. She wondered who it was who had spoken in such an upset and anxious way. Could it be the doctor's wife? But somehow Helen thought not. And who was Miss Emma, and what was all that about running away?

She had been shown into a pleasant large room, with patterned carpet and heavy brown curtains; its row of hard chairs showed it to be the waiting room, but the severity of the furniture was tempered by the thick oak table covered with magazines and the pictures and posters on the walls. At the end of the room

12

were rows of filing cabinets and a table and typewriter. After her strange reception she felt more apprehensive than ever, her pleasure at the aspect outside the house evaporating into fears at the aura of anxiety inside.

The sound of voices came to her from the hall. 'It's all right Mrs Rose, she had only got as far as the market. Ken Palmer on the vegetable stall saw her and kept her talking until I arrived. I've taken her back to school. You say Miss Wainwright is here? Ask her to wait five minutes and then bring her into my room please.'

These words, spoken in a deep, quick, assured voice did not help to allay Helen's confusion. Was the owner of the voice as severe and hard as he sounded. The harrassed Mrs Rose appeared in the doorway, but this time she looked a little less bothered and she was apologetic as she spoke.

'I'm sorry to keep you waiting, Miss, and for being upset when you arrived but you see it's Miss Emma . . . but there, I mustn't say any more, or Doctor will be cross with me and he will want to tell you himself in any case. You come with me and I'll show where his room is.'

All thoughts of composure left Helen as she followed the woman out of the waiting-room. Across the hall was a passage with two white-painted doors; the first one was open and standing outside was a tall figure, dark hair with flecks of grey, his lined, serious face not smiling as he put out his hand to greet Helen. As she felt the firm grip of his handshake she pulled herself together. Meeting his direct gaze she had the impression of a steely, guarded appraisal. With her long dark hair just touching the jacket of her warm woollen suit of soft red, she felt she was looking at her best, and she returned the handshake with a confidence that had been ebbing away ever since she had stepped inside the front door.

'Miss Wainwright?' enquired the deep, assured voice. 'I am Mark Sinclair. This is Mrs Rose, my housekeeper.' He turned to the older woman. 'Mrs Rose perhaps you would be good enough to bring us some coffee. I am sure Miss Wainwright would welcome a hot drink after her long journey.'

At the formal introduction, Mrs Rose smiled faintly and without saying anything, turned and went back to the direction of the hall, returning shortly with the requested coffee.

In spite of his serious expression, the doctor seemed to be doing his best to be putting her at ease and she was surprised when he indicated a chair in front of his consulting table and drew himself one up beside her, not sitting behind the table as she had expected would be the case in a formal interview. She felt herself relaxing until she heard his first words.

'I am going to be honest with you. I know

14

that you can type and that you have been a receptionist in London. But that is what bothers me. I don't want a girl who yearns for a London night life. She won't get it here. Garthdale is entirely agricultural and rural and Hexton, although it is the largest town in the dale, is still no more than a quiet market town. There are no cinemas or theatres nearer than Leeds.' He gave her a keen look as though trying to read her thoughts. 'I'll be even more honest with you. Yours was the only application we had, which is the reason why I've brought you all the way from London. It seems these days that girls are flocking to the cities away from the towns. All the local girls here cannot wait to get into Leeds to work in spite of the long bus journey every day.' He stopped abruptly as though he didn't usually say so much. 'Now you tell me what made you send in an application.'

Helen took a deep breath, and tried to find some semblance of courage. It had to be the truth. 'I was like that too; I lived in Dorset all my life and couldn't wait to get a job in London. I've been there nearly three years and as the time goes on, I just keep wishing for the sight of a field, for open spaces, just to be away from the sprawl of buildings, the traffic, the rush. I suppose the truth is I'm not a city girl.' It sounded so weak, so feeble, she could hardly mention the heartache that Jeremy had brought into her life. She looked up at the man

15

at her side and surprisingly the undeniably good-looking face was sympathetic as he slowly nodded his head.

'Believe it or not I know how you feel. My first practice was in the middle of Manchester and after a few years I couldn't wait to . . .' A mask came over his face, his eyes hardened, his hand was raised to his head as though to try and conceal some difficult hidden memory.

'However,' he resumed, 'you seem to be the sensible kind of girl we look for in a busy surgery. You are used to having a lot of people around you, and your London office must have been a busy one. I'm willing to offer you the job on a three months' trial—that is, trial on both sides. Now I will tell you what is involved and then perhaps you will have a better idea of what life is about up here.'

She sat quietly and still while he explained that he was the main partner in the practice. Dr Wharton, although the senior, was partly retired and had surgeries only twice a week; they shared weekend duties. They had no dispensary as there was a good chemist in the square. She would have weekends off but would be expected to work for one hour on Saturday mornings for the emergency surgery; compensating for this she would have every Wednesday afternoon off as there was no surgery then. On other days there were two surgeries, one at 8.30 and one at 4.30. She would stay until all the patients had gone after the 4.30 surgery, but the time after lunch would be her own. If she took the job he would arrange for the present receptionist, Sheila Hembury, who was leaving to have a baby, to stay on for a few days to show her the duties.

When he finished talking there was a silence. Although Helen felt she should have been prepared for a great difference between this and her 9–5 London office job, she found it hard to take in all that he was telling her. At the back of her mind the name Emma kept making itself heard. Miss Emma, Mrs Rose had said, running away. Yet Dr Sinclair had not mentioned her.

He broke the silence 'You don't seem to have much to say. Perhaps it's not what you expected. I'll ask Mrs Rose to show you round the house, and if you like it and the accommodation we have to offer you, before you come to a final decision there is something else I will have to explain to you.'

'Thank you' she managed to say, but still seemed too tongue-tied. She thought it must be the hint that there was some difficulty here that she had not yet learned about.

He took her out of the consulting-room, through the hall and to the back of the house where she found herself in an enormous kitchen. It was fully equipped with modern units but gave the comfortable impression of the old family living kitchen of years gone by. There was an oak table and chairs, a heavy

17

dresser, a couple of easy chairs and an Aga range placed beside a modern electric cooker.

'Show Miss Wainwright round, Mrs Rose. She would particularly like to see the room she would have if she came to us.' He disappeared back into the consulting-room and Helen was left with Mrs Rose, who now seemed to be more relaxed than at first. She wasn't tall, and her lined face and white hair set close in soft waves gave the intimation of firmness, and her eyes as they looked at Helen held a kindly expression.

'Well dear, this is the kitchen, we eat in here and it's really my sitting-room as well. The dining room we don't use much, Doctor says it's too formal, but he does have friends to dinner once in a while.'

'Do you do the cooking?' Helen enquired.

'Yes, I suppose I'm what you'd call a cook-housekeeper. I do the shopping as well, though the groceries are delivered every week so that saves me.' She walked out into the hall towards the wide staircase. 'I'll show you your room now.'

Upstairs five doors led off a broad landing, and Mrs Rose opened the far door and Helen followed her into a large room. She gave a gasp of delight.

'Oh, what a lovely room' she said wonderingly. And indeed it was. It was a spacious room, not just the bedroom that Helen had expected, but a dream bed-sitting room for any girl. It had a single bed in the corner with a flowered coverlet in the same material as the curtains, an easy chair, and another chair set against a small handsome oak table; in the other corner were a wash-basin and work-top, with an electric kettle and a toaster. A large wardrobe and dressing table were in the same wood as the writing-table; underneath the window was a television set.

'It's got everything,' gasped Helen. 'Did you choose it all Mrs Rose?'

'Oh, no, it was the doctor. He's very thoughtful even though he has got so much on his mind.'

Helen had by this time moved over to the window and the view increased her sense of joy and pleasure. She looked at the gardens and trees, and the rooftops of the old town, but unlike the closed in suffocating feeling she had from her London window, here was space and distance, and green and sky. She stared and stared; she was looking right down Garthdale to the hills beyond, and beyond that, slim and blue in the distance, yet another fold of hills. She suddenly had a strong inner conviction that this was where she wanted to be and she turned to Mrs Rose.

'It's all beautiful,' she sighed. 'I would feel very lucky if I could come here.'

'Well, to be sure, I hope you do; it's not a happy house but you would have everything you wanted.'

Again that hint of something wrong, the same suggestion of trouble that had been in Dr Sinclair's first words that she had overheard when she arrived.

Out on the landing, Mrs Rose pointed to the far door. 'That's the Doctor's, and those are the stairs up to the attics. Two nice long bedrooms there are, but not used at the moment, only for storing things. This next room to yours is Miss Emma's.'

This time Helen could not keep back the words, the question.

'But, Mrs Rose, who is Emma; I've heard her mentioned so many times since I've been here but I still seem to be in the dark.'

The older woman looked askance. 'Do you mean to tell me the doctor hasn't told you about Miss Emma? She's his young daughter, but ...' She broke off when she saw the consternation in Helen's face. Consternation that covered a multitude of feelings as Helen looked at Mrs Rose. Helen had somehow had the idea that Doctor Sinclair was unmarried, there had been no mention of a Mrs Sinclair.

Mrs Rose could be heard almost talking to herself. 'Perhaps he meant me to tell her—perhaps she won't come when she knows the trouble there's been.'

'Please tell me if there is something I should know. I can't help feeling that ...'

'Miss Wainwright.' Her words were cut short by the voice of Dr Sinclair from the foot of the

20

stairs. 'If you have finished looking round I will show you a bit of Hexton to give you some idea of what kind of town it is.'

Helen walked slowly downstairs, her thoughts in a whirl. She joined the tall figure of the doctor, now wearing a sheepskin jacket over his suit, and he guided her to the front door. Once outside they did not turn towards the market square but walked in silence in the other direction to the bridge.

As they reached the other side of the river and stood beside a stone stile which led into a large field, Helen looked around her and what she saw filled her with a sense of great beauty and belonging. The river was not deep, its waters rushed and bubbled over the stones, and glinted in the afternoon light. She could have listened to it for ever; it did indeed seem to be the sound of eternity. She took her eyes from the water and looked up the dale at the low pastures lying each side of the tree-lined river, the hills rising steeply and on the fells on either side, grey farms and cottages, alone or grouped together in tiny hamlets. In the distance the dale head enclosed the narrowing river and the hills beyond gave further promises of serenity and beauty. She was looking at a whole community, the little town at one end, the villages, the farms, the river winding through and giving the dale its name. As though reading her thoughts Dr Sinclair looked at her and said quietly: 'That is

Garthdale. I wanted you to see it.'

Helen turned her head at his softly spoken words, his tone had been unusually gentle. Had she but known it her face as her eyes met his was also gentle, no longer on edge but naturally eager, her expression shining and lovely.

He led the way through the stile and into the meadow. 'We'll walk along the river for a way, I have something to tell you. To ask you.'

Now the truth is coming, thought Helen, but whatever it is, it can't make me give this up if I am offered it.

The doctor continued to speak. His tone was quiet, he chose his words carefully. As they walked along that beautiful stretch of water Helen learned the truth about Emma. She was Dr Sinclair's young daughter, only 8 years old. She had been born in Manchester and when she was four years old the family had moved to the Hexton practice. From the start things went wrong, Mrs Sinclair did not like the small country town and spent most of her time in Leeds and on long visits back to Manchester. Emma was left in the charge of various au-pair girls who never stayed very long, and gradually Emma became very difficult and naughty.

'I must tell you that in the end Louise, my wife, left me and we were divorced a year later.' The words were bitter and filled with remorse. 'I should never have brought her here.'

He went on to tell Helen how Emma had idolised her beautiful mother and had never seemed to recover from the shock of the break-up of the marriage. His wife wanted to be free of her parental ties, had given up all rights to her child to the doctor, and had then re-married and gone to live in Canada.

'We stopped having the au-pair girls, and I got Mrs Rose to live in, and for a time things improved. But this last year has been really difficult. Emma keeps running away from school, she disrupts the class, and shows nothing but animosity, even violence towards the other children. Mrs Rose does her best but she is not getting any younger, and not long ago her sister was widowed and Mrs Rose visits her at the weekends. Sheila Hembury has done her best too, but she has her own home to think about and now she is expecting the baby.'

Helen was silent; they had stopped and stood staring into the ever tumbling water. 'Why are you telling me all this, Dr Sinclair?'

'Miss Wainwright, I will be completely open with you and tell you that you seem to be exactly the kind of person I am looking for. The duties in the surgery are not arduous as we are a small practice, though I am myself kept very busy.' He turned to face her. 'If you come, I would also ask you to help me with Emma.'

Helen was dumbfounded 'But how could I help? I'm not used to any children, let alone one who is as disturbed as Emma seems to be.'

He paused. 'At the moment she is surrounded by older people and I'm afraid I am often called out when I need to be there. I want a young person—not to take responsibility for her, that is mine. But to be there in little ways, to meet her from school, perhaps take her out sometimes, to read to her or play a game in the evenings.' A sorrowful, worried look came over his face. 'I suppose I am asking the impossible, but I am going to ask you if you will come as my receptionist and at the same time help me out with Emma. Don't answer straight away. We will walk back to the house, have a quick look at Hexton, and then go and meet Emma from school. You will have time to think it over and when you have met her you can give me your answer.'

They turned and walked silently back along the river. Crossing the bridge, a large van came up behind them. Helen felt a firm hand on her shoulder holding her back. His touch was one of politeness, but the feeling of it swept right through her, the unexpected confusion of her sensations adding to the tumult of her mind. She felt torn in two. In spite of his seriousness she liked Dr Sinclair, and she loved the house, her room and this prospect of living in such a lovely part of Yorkshire. But she had been honest when she had said she had never had contact with children, apart from her own nephews and nieces, her sister's children who were still only toddlers. It was not what she had expected. Could she do it? The questions raced round in her mind and by the time they had walked round the square and reached Bridge House she had no idea what answer she was going to give.

'We will fetch your things from Mrs Rose and then go to the school. By the time the children come out, it will be time for you to get the bus back to Leeds.'

He waited while she fetched her bag and said goodbye to Mrs Rose, then they made their way across the top of the square, turning into the road that led up the dale to Garth Head. The school was typical of the village schools of the area, solid stone buildings with their small playgrounds and lovely back-cloth of fields and fells.

Several mothers were already waiting outside and spoke to Dr Sinclair. He nodded but did not speak. Helen nervously stood by his side not knowing what to say, not knowing what to expect. After what seemed an age the children started to come out. Helen glanced at each little girl thinking she would see a dark-haired version of her father, but when a small tiny-faced fair-haired child stopped in front of them, Helen guessed that Emma was like her mother in looks. There was no smile from the child.

'Hello, Daddy. Where's Mrs Rose?'

The doctor took Helen's arm. 'Emma I want you to meet Miss Wainwright. I am hoping she is going to be my new receptionist and come to live at Bridge House.'

The child straightened up, a wilful obstinate look of pure dislike coming into her face. She came up, and to Helen's dismay and horror shouted out: 'I don't want you. I don't like you. I only want my Mummy!' and turning she went running away from them in the direction of the square.

When Helen saw Dr Sinclair's expression, she was shocked by the misery, perplexity and appeal in his eyes. He caught her hand. 'I must run after Emma. Please say you will come. I do need you.'

Caution, reason and common sense flew with the wind as she met his anguished look, and she could only see the desperation in his eyes and the fair curls of the running child.

'Yes.' She almost shouted it. 'Yes, I will come.'

A quick press of the hand and he was chasing down the road after Emma, leaving Helen to shake her head and make her way slowly in disbelief to the bus and to London; to a long journey during which the words 'I don't want you, I want my Mummy' kept ringing through her head, immediately to be echoed by the heartfelt plea of the forlorn doctor 'I do need you.'

26

# CHAPTER TWO

The next four weeks had an unreal quality about them. Helen had written to Dr Sinclair to accept the post and had received a short letter in reply confirming the date that she would start, the first of March. During those weeks she worked hard, it being a busy time of year for an estate agent; she had to get used to seeing Jeremy every day and maintaining a distant businesslike manner in his presence, subduing the feelings that engulfed her when he stood near her or spoke to her. It helped that she had the prospect of Garthdale ever before her. The problem of Emma she refused to consider, since she could do nothing by worrying about it; she would have to rely on her commonsense and sympathetic nature to cope with the difficulties when she moved to Bridge House. There were practical details to see to, such as finding another girl to share the flat with Jenny, who was full of curiosity about the situation in Hexton and determined to match-make between Helen and Dr Sinclair, until in the end her cheerful chatter began to tell on Helen's nerves. She started to count the days until she would be able to settle into that room of her own with its lovely view.

She also had a lot of sorting out to do, as she had been in the flat nearly three years and had gathered together what she thought of as a lot of clutter. All her kitchen pans, china and utensils she decided to sell to the girl who was coming in as she would not need them in Hexton. She had nowhere to store them; if she ever had a flat of her own again, she would have to make a fresh start. By the end of February she had packed her largest suitcase and sent it on ahead of her, leaving a small case and bag to carry on her journey north.

For the second time she made the long train journey to Leeds, having confirmed with Dr Sinclair that her travel arrangements would be convenient. This time she travelled at a weekend as she had finished at Sadlers on a Friday. As she went through the barrier and was preparing herself to carry her luggage to the bus station, she was stopped by a familiar figure looking just as he had when she had last seen him running down the road after Emma.

'Dr Sinclair!' she could not keep the pleasure from her voice.

His manner was serious as before, and the lines of his face seemed etched with care, but his reply was pleasant enough. 'I thought you might have a lot of luggage and a Saturday is always busy on the bus. Dr Wharton is doing the calls for me. The car is parked outside.' He took her case and bag and she followed him into the station forecourt, settling beside him in the Range Rover she had noticed parked outside Bridge House. It was a quiet drive to

Hexton. Helen did not like to ask about Emma and Dr Sinclair did not volunteer any information.

When they arrived at Bridge House Mrs Rose was there to greet her enthusiastically. 'I'll make you a cup of tea before you go up to your room. Come in the kitchen.' The big room was warm and welcoming with the homely smell of fresh baking. On the table were racks of tea-cakes, scones and buns, and an enormous fruit cake as well as some delicious looking fruit pies.

'Saturday's my baking day,' Helen was told as she sat down at the table. Mrs Rose was much more friendly than she had remembered: perhaps Helen had been more worried than she had realised on the day of her interview. That day made her think of Emma and as though reading her thoughts, Mrs Rose's next remark was about the little girl.

'I'm surprised that Miss Emma's not here begging for a bun or a curranty that I always make for her from the scraps of pastry. I haven't seen her since lunchtime. There's no doubt she'll be up in her room reading. Very quiet she's been since you were here last. Not been so much trouble either. I was thinking it was because she was looking forward to having someone younger in the house. It weren't right for her to have just the Doctor and me for company.'

It was obvious that Dr Sinclair had not told his housekeeper about the scene at the school, and Helen stayed silent. Mrs Rose seemed to relish having someone to talk to and continued to tell Helen all about Emma, though Helen listened rather guiltily, feeling that Mrs Rose shouldn't be telling her all this, yet at the same time not being able to curb her curiosity into the background of Emma's life.

'Her mother's to blame for it all. Neglected the poor child was, from the minute the family moved from Manchester. The Doctor that busy, and *her*' (in Mrs Rose's eyes Dr Sinclair's wife was always *her*) 'for ever off to Leeds, or back to Manchester to see her old friends. Left Miss Emma with them au-pair girls, 'tweren't no life for a child. And she was starting school as well, never did settle, not surprising when you reason it out. Her mother not there and her father always busy, she spent all her time with them girls as couldn't even speak proper English. Don't think I was here then because I wasn't. But everyone in Hexton knew what was going on. They liked Doctor well enough, but didn't have no time for her. Always off gallivanting with her boyfriends, 'tweren't surprising she went off altogether in the end, and then there was the divorce. Shouldn't happen to a doctor. Doesn't do him any good.'

Mrs Rose was in full flow by this time, enjoying the chance to tell someone the whole sorry story. The guilt again crept over Helen but once more she allowed her curiosity to get the better of her and she let Mrs Rose continue.

'That's as when I came. He stopped having them girls and I always lived in. But it didn't make Miss Emma any better. Worse she got. Missed her mother. Her was a lovely lady when all's said and done and Miss Emma idolised her in spite of hardly ever seeing her. Broke the child's heart when her mother took off. That were over two years ago, she has settled down, but she's easily upset and that's when she runs away from school and plays them up. I do what I can for her but it's a young face she needs, not old bones like me.' She looked Helen straight in the eyes. 'I was pleased when the Doctor decided to have someone to live in when Sheila goes. You look a sensible sort, perhaps you'll succeed where Doctor and I have failed.'

Helen didn't know what to say. 'She may resent me at first,' she said slowly. 'She probably still misses her mother even after all this time. I told Dr Sinclair I hadn't had a lot of experience of children but I'm willing to try.' She paused, thinking of what Mrs Rose had told her; the story was a sad one but she was glad she knew it; she was sure it would help her in understanding any difficulties she might have with Emma. 'Perhaps I'll go and unpack now and then I can meet Emma later on.'

31

Mrs Rose nodded 'Yes, your big case has arrived and we put it in your room. You can find your way can't you? I'll finish clearing up in here.'

Helen walked upstairs, Mrs Rose's words still ringing in her ears. She wondered if she could succeed with such a disturbed child. She felt very sorry for Emma and gave herself a mental shake, determined to do all she could to make life happier for her. Little did she realise that her resolve was to be put to the test so quickly.

As she reached the top of the stairs and looked across the wide landing towards her room she saw a small figure crouching at the foot of the door. She stopped. Cosily dressed in blue jeans and a thick red polo-necked jumper which heightened the brightness and fairness of her curls, for a moment Emma looked the picture of a small eight year old waiting patiently for something nice to happen. Then Helen saw the expression on the girl's face, the mouth set in a scowl, the eyes looking towards the stairs and now in Helen's direction, full of hostility and dislike. Her hands were clenched, her whole body was rigid.

Helen went slowly towards the room. Emma didn't move.

Behave normally, whispered a voice inside Helen. She mustn't show her she had no idea how to deal with a rebellious child, even though she felt as though she towered above Emma in a totally menacing way. Perhaps, subconsciously, the thought precipitated the deed, for the next moment she found herself sitting on the floor beside the small girl. There was silence for a long time. Puzzlement had crept into Emma's face but the scowl remained. At last Helen said quietly, 'Are you going to let me go into my room, Emma?' She triggered off an instant and violent response, the words coming shrilly and not hiding the very depth of her feeling and the meaning behind her action.

'It's not your room. It's my mummy's room and you're not going in it.' A rush of understanding and at the same time a subdued fury swept through Helen. When Dr Sinclair had decided to have a receptionist who lived in, he had obviously decorated and furnished his wife's old room. Emma must have seen all the changes that were being made, and the last link with her mother was taken away from her. Her resentment and hurt had built up against the person who was going to have that room, built up and manifested itself in the screamed out words at the school a month ago, and now in this mutinous behaviour outside what she still thought of as her mother's door.

Helen understood how the still grieving Emma felt. For grief it was—the loss of a loved one can play havoc with young emotions, and here was Emma, for two years having mourned

33

the loss of her mother. Helen's inner fury increased. What kind of woman must the ex-Mrs Sinclair have been, to have abandoned her young daughter so finally? Mrs Rose had not said if she had ever come over from Canada on a visit. When Helen thought of the story she had so guiltily listened to, she now realised forcefully that her inner feeling had been right when it told her that she ought to know. But now, to know and understand was one thing, to act and do the right thing was another. From the recesses of her mind came an idea that she had read somewhere, that the easiest way to deal with a difficult or naughty child was to distract her. She found herself saying: 'Emma, my big case has been put in my room with all my things in it. Would you like to help me unpack? Perhaps you could find a place for them to go.' She watched a struggle going on in Emma's face. The frown stayed, but it was one of someone making a decision, not one of bad-temper.

'Have you got any dogs?'

'Dogs? Oh, you mean ornaments. I'm not sure. There's a cat and I've got a furry dog. He sleeps on my bed.'

These last words acted as a miraculous password; scowl and frown disappeared, there was no smile but the glowering look had changed to one of interest and curiosity.

'All right then. Can I really help you unpack?'

'Yes, of course you can. Up you get and we'll go and unlock the cases.' Helen leaned over and opened the door of the comfortable room. Emma looked round as though summing it up. 'It's not so pretty as it was when Mummy was here, but there's a book case. Have you got any books?'

'I've got lots of books but I don't think they would do for you. Do you like reading?'

'Yes I do. I read all the time but I haven't got enough books. I get some from school but we are only allowed one at a time.' This was quite a long sentence, thought Helen, we seem to have broken the ice, and she made a mental note to find out if there was a library she could take Emma to. She did not expect to find a bookshop in a place the size of Hexton.

'We'll have to see what we can do about that,' she told Emma. 'Now, what about that case? Here it is. I'll unlock and you can help me.' There followed an unexpectedly enjoyable half-hour. Children do not store up resentment for long, and soon, with her interest captured, Emma was taking things out of the case faster than Helen could find places for them. The box of ornaments was found and with squeals of delight Emma placed the little animals and birds on top of the bookcase. Then she gave a shout. 'I've found furry dog.' She hugged the animal to her and Helen watched the small face change. Gone was the look of hatred which she had encountered as

35

she had climbed the stairs. For the first time a smile lit up Emma's face and transformed it. Helen swallowed, the furry dog was 'Moocher' and she had had him ever since she could remember. He was threadbare in parts, but still beloved. He had always sat on Helen's bed, but now she looked at him and remembered her age, then thought of Emma's need and told herself not to be silly and sentimental.

'His name is Moocher. Would you like him to go on your bed, Emma?' Before there was time for a reply, a loud voice called from the bottom of the stairs.

'Emma, where are you?'

Helen watched with astonishment at the transformation back from the smiling child to the old white, strained hostile expression.

'It's Maxine.' whispered Emma.

'Who's Maxine?' Helen enquired.

'She's Daddy's friend.' Another whisper. 'I don't like her.' The strident voice came again: 'Emma, I'm calling you. What are you doing?' Emma walked slowly to the door and went out onto the landing, still clutching the dog. Helen stood in the doorway wondering who could be the owner of such an imperious voice. As Emma reached the bottom of the stairs, Helen heard the voice again.

'Whatever have you got there?'

'It—it's Moocher.'

'But it's nothing but a scruffy woollen dog.

Where did you get it?'

'He's mine,' faltered Emma. 'Helen gave him to me.'

By this time, Helen felt she should make herself known and went down the stairs not knowing quite what to expect. When she saw the figure standing there she experienced an immediate inward impact of dislike. Here was a woman who knew how to dress and who dressed in style. Expensive brown suit of fine wool, a warm jacket slung carelessly over her shoulders, cream silk scarf tied around her neck. Her hair was an indeterminate shade of light brown, but beautifully cut and shaped about her handsome head. She wore a gold brooch on her jacket and two gold bracelets round her slim wrists. Her features were striking too, large brown eyes and delicately arched brows, cheeks and chin which were finely and firmly moulded. Only one thing spoiled the classic beauty: the mouth was thin and contradicted the generosity of line that the rest of the face carried.

By the time this instant impression had implanted itself, Helen had reached the hall and stood by Emma's side. The cool eyes seemed to sum her up and immediately dismiss her.

'I suppose you are Miss Wainwright. Mark told me you were coming today, he said he was going to Leeds to meet you. I had expected him to have lunch with me as we often do on

Saturdays.'

Helen had expected to shake hands but no such friendly gesture was proffered. She was still completely at sea, but she was not left to wonder for long. The cool voice assailed her again.

'I don't suppose Mark has had time to tell you about me. I am Maxine Graham, I have a craft shop and art gallery in the town. I have known him a long time.' The implication was that she had known him very well for a long time. 'As I did not see him for lunch I popped in to arrange our outing tomorrow. We are going to take Emma to Harrogate.'

Helen was beginning to recognise the different expressions that Emma could produce even though she had only known the child a few hours. Obstinacy was in her face this time.

'I don't want to go with you,' she objected.

'It's not what you want, it's what your father says,' snapped Maxine. 'You know very well that Mrs Rose has her day off on Sunday, to go and visit her sister, and that you come with us if we go out.' Somehow Maxine managed to make it sound as though the last thing she wanted was to have Emma in tow, and that she was completely dominated by Mark.

Helen looked from the haughty woman to the small child still clutching the furry dog. Here was yet another tension in Emma's life, touching her father rather than herself, but explaining a lot of Emma's present unhappiness.

'I'm afraid I don't know where Dr Sinclair is.' Helen started to say.

'Don't worry, I'll go and leave a message with Mrs Rose.' Maxine disappeared into the kitchen.

Helen turned to Emma. 'Shall we finish my room now?' she asked her, but got only a gruff reply.

'No, she's spoiled it. I'm going to take Moocher to my room. You did say I could have him, didn't you?' There was appeal and longing in her voice.

Helen sighed. 'Yes, you can have him, Emma.'

They both went upstairs, Helen to finish her unpacking and straighten her room, having many things to think about and ponder over. She had only been in Bridge House for two hours but seemed to have unearthed a Pandora's box of complicated feelings and emotions. She looked out of her window at the peaceful hills in the fading sunshine of a winter afternoon and thought how they contrasted with the turmoil in the house. She had seemed to be making some progress with Emma until the appearance on the scene of Maxine Graham. What did the dominating woman mean in the doctor's life; why did Emma dislike her so much? Helen felt she had a lot to learn and as she looked at the hills it was as though their permanence might somehow give her strength and understanding.

The rest of the day was to pass quietly. Mark Sinclair had not returned when Helen sat down with Mrs Rose and Emma to an old-fashioned high tea. Emma was quiet and Helen felt tired. She watched Emma go upstairs with Mrs Rose to her usual lonely bed-time routine and the make-believe world of her books.

The next day Helen was glad to have to herself, though she did meet Dr Sinclair when she found her way down to the kitchen to do herself a late breakfast. He was preparing for his trip to Harrogate with Maxine Graham and Emma, and as Helen entered the room she was surprised to be greeted by a warm smile which lit up his normally serious face, reaching his eyes and giving him a devastating attraction of which she had previously been unaware.

She stood still as he walked towards her holding out his hand. 'Helen,' he said, still smiling, 'I can't go on calling you Miss Wainwright when I've heard nothing but Helen this and Helen that from Emma this morning—you have made a good start there. Here is something I'd forgotten to tell you about.'

She held her breath as he took her hand and dropped something into it, thrilled not only at the touch, but at the realization that what he had given her were the keys to a car. He had asked her at the interview if she could drive and she had thought it nothing but a routine question; now she looked at him with enquiry in her eyes, and he quickly answered her look of anticipation. 'My main car is the Range Rover, but I've also got a Mini. Sheila used to use it for taking out prescriptions and doing odd errands, but now I want you to regard it as your car.'

Her delight and astonishment cut him short. 'I don't know how to thank you, Dr Sinclair . . .'

'Mark,' he corrected. 'We are not going to be formal.'

'Er . . . Mark. I really wasn't expecting to have a car—it's absolutely wonderful.' She hesitated before asking, 'Do you mean I can use it in my free time?'

He nodded his head in assent. 'Yes, that is what I do mean, and I hope you will see something of the Dales when you have time and . . .' What he was going to say was never known as a loud call came from the front door. It was Maxine.

'Mark, are you never coming? Emma and I are waiting in the car.' Mark looked at Helen. 'I'd better go. The Mini is in the garage. Enjoy yourself.' She watched him hurry off and found herself clutching the keys as though she couldn't believe her luck. She spent the rest of the morning looking at the maps which the doctor had thoughtfully placed on her bookshelf.

She got the Mini out of the garage in the afternoon and drove around Hexton to try it out. Then she set off to the next dale, Wedderdale, taking the road over the bridge which wound slowly up to the top of the moor. Here she could not resist getting out and enjoying the exhilarating air and views which were all so new to her. Her whole being was filled with a sense of happiness and good fortune that this wonderful place was to become her home. Back in the car a similar road with its steep bends took her into Wedderdale. This valley was on a grander scale than Garthdale and attracted more visitors, particularly in the market town of Hesketh which dominated the entrance to the dale. The river was broad, with lovely walks through the trees on either side. The old town had become a popular haunt for the curio and antique hunter, and Helen spent a happy hour walking through the streets with their cobbled slopes, looking in the shop windows. At this time of year the town was not crowded and her sense of leisure and well-being increased as she strolled about, before taking the car back over the hill to Hexton.

Back at Bridge House she had her tea on her own as Mrs Rose had not yet returned, and in the evening Emma came home sulky and evasive with few words for Helen. Mark, after helping Emma to bed, his usual Sunday routine, retired to his consulting room and gave Helen no further chance for conversation, except to tell her that next morning he had arranged for Sheila Hembury to come back for one day to help Helen find her way about the routine of the waiting-room and the reception desk.

Monday morning found Helen at her desk in good time. First appointments were at 9 o'clock but the phone started ringing at eight-thirty and Helen was to feel glad of Sheila's guidance and assistance. The two were the same age, Sheila happy and relaxed in her pregnancy and not sorry to be taking life a bit more easily as the months swiftly progressed. They worked well together, Helen learning quickly and getting used to being an object of curiosity to the first patients that she was to meet.

'I'm sure that half of them have invented ailments just to come and see what you are like,' joked Sheila when they were having a well-earned coffee break at the end of the rush. 'Monday morning is always busy but it seemed twice as bad this morning. Do you think you can manage on your own this evening? Mark has asked me to come in again for one more morning, but I think he wanted you to find your own feet as soon as possible.'

Helen noticed that Sheila seemed to have a very good and easy relationship with the doctor, and as though following Helen's line of thought the former receptionist was keen to put in a good word for her employer.

'How are you getting on with Mark? I expect you will find him a bit stiff at first, but there's not a person I'd sooner go to if I was in trouble. And he's got his own problems too.' She almost repeated Mrs Rose's words, but unlike the housekeeper was not going to betray confidences and spread gossip about the family. 'I think I will leave you to put the notes away. Officially the surgery closes from twelve to four, but you may get the occasional emergency. I used to go home after morning surgery and come back at four o'clock. Mrs Rose is always here to answer any phone calls and to take messages.' Helen thanked her very much, she was glad to meet someone her own age and appreciated Sheila's friendliness and help.

Emma stayed to school dinner, so a quick lunch was shared with Mrs Rose. They were chatting and washing up together, when the phone rang from the waiting room. Helen hurried in to answer it, a frown coming to her face as she listened to the voice at the other end who asked to speak to Sheila.

'I'm afraid Sheila has left. This is Helen Wainwright. Can I help you?'

'Oh, Miss Wainwright, I didn't realise that you had already arrived. This is Neil Brandon, headmaster of Hexton Primary School. I don't know how much Dr Sinclair has told you about

44

Emma, but I'm afraid she's missing again. Can you tell Dr Sinclair if he is there, though he is probably on his rounds by now. Mrs Rose will know what to do. We've started looking here; if you could come round I'll meet you at the school gate.' He rang off as Mrs Rose came hurrying from the kitchen.

'It's never Miss Emma again. And your first day too. I might have known it would happen. It's nearly every time when that Mrs Graham and the Doctor have taken her out for the day. Seems to upset her something dreadful. You go round to the school and I'll stay here, in case she makes her way home straight away. Mr Brandon will tell you where to look. You'll like him. All the children do, and the parents. A good head-teacher he is.'

Helen had been putting her coat on while Mrs Rose was talking, and had run down the steps of Bridge House. It was only five minutes to the school and there by the gate stood the man who must be Neil Brandon.

He smiled at her and took her hand. 'I'm sorry this should happen on your first day. Emma has been difficult all the morning and although we tried to keep an eye on her when they were out playing after dinner, when the whistle went and they lined up her teacher realised she was missing. Jane Elstow is her teacher, and she's out hunting for Emma now.'

Helen liked his open-ness, the feeling of capability that came with his strong figure. Of medium height, with a shock of curly, sandy hair he was not good-looking in the traditional sense, but had pleasant features and clear candid blue eyes, which gave him an attractiveness which appealed to her immediately.

She followed him through the playground, now empty of children, to the field which adjoined it. Obviously used for the boys' football, the grass was cut short and it was bordered by a tall hedge, here and there showing the first few spikes of the fresh green of early spring. Walking along the hedge on one side of the field was a short figure, evidently the teacher that Neil Brandon had mentioned. As he and Helen made their way towards her, he said 'Jane is looking in all the usual hiding places. It's the hedge that causes us the trouble; it can easily be reached from the playground and here and there it has small gaps just big enough for a child to squeeze through. On the other side is the lane that leads into the square, but sometimes Emma will just hide in the hedge until she is found.'

They had reached Miss Elstow by this time and introductions were made. Helen was given the impression of a sensible girl in her early twenties, with serious mouth and eyes, her outstanding feature being her fair, golden hair which she wore swept back off her face and falling long and shining down her back. She greeted Helen cheerfully. 'I am glad you have come to Bridge House. Emma is a very intelligent child and I think it will help her to have someone younger around her.' She echoed what Mrs Rose had said earlier. 'Running away from school is becoming quite a problem. Sometimes we find her curled up in the hedge. She is very quick to take the opportunity if she sees the person on playground duty looking the other way for a moment; it's just as though it is the attention she is looking for rather than a dislike of school and a need to run away.' She turned to the headmaster. 'Shall I go back to the class now, Neil, and leave you and Miss Wainwright to continue searching?'

Helen looked at Neil Brandon and spoke for the first time. 'Where are the usual places to look?'

'We'd better go down the lane,' he replied, 'and have a look in the square. There is no market today so she won't be at the stalls which is one of her favourite places; or she may have already gone home.'

He led her across the playground and down the lane that ran along the side of the school. It seemed to Helen that neither he nor Miss Elstow were particularly worried, but she supposed that by now they must have become accustomed to Emma's disappearances.

As they turned from the lane into the square Neil touched Helen's arm.

'Look' he said, and pointed to two figures

walking along Bridge Street.

'Oh, there she is.' Helen breathed a sigh of relief. Mrs Rose was walking towards them with a reluctant and sullen Emma pulling at her hand. Helen was at a loss for words. Should she be cross with the child, or not make too much fuss to avoid highlighting Emma's escapade? She did not have to worry, Neil was very much in control as the pair reached him.

'Emma, I hope that this is the last time we have this nonsense. You know very well the anxiety that is caused when you run off.' The little girl was silent and looked at the ground, still holding Mrs Rose's hand. 'Now that Miss Wainwright has come, you will have someone to talk to and to play with you; if you will let her she will be a good friend to you.' Stubbornness was still written all over the youngster's face: 'I don't want Helen, I want my ...' Then she broke off suddenly, as looking at Helen she realised that it was not anger and crossness she saw, but the same kind expression she had seen when Helen arrived and she had helped to unpack the case. As Emma hesitated, Helen decided on firmness. 'Emma, it was very silly of you to run away when you knew I was going to meet you from school. We will take you back to your class now and I will be there at the school gate later on this afternoon.'

Doubt struggled with rebellion in the small

face, then Emma took her hand from Mrs Rose and reluctantly took Helen's.

'All right,' she muttered, then as though her capitulation deserved a reward she looked up at Helen and said 'Will you read me a story tonight?' Helen was still firm. 'No, not tonight. It will be straight to bed after tea. But when Mr Brandon tells me you have been behaving yourself at school and not trying to run away, then we'll begin to think about a game or a story at bedtime.' She knew it was bribery, but felt that perhaps a reward for good behaviour was not a bad thing.

They were arriving back at the school and Helen was taken into the classroom, while Emma slipped quietly back to her table. Once outside, the headmaster turned to Helen. 'Come into my office. I think a short chat about Emma would not do any harm. And please call me Neil, I am sure we are going to be seeing too much of each other to be on formal terms.'

As she sat by his desk, he gave her a smile and said 'Crisis over once again. Helen, I'm going to be very frank with you. Nothing else will do. I've known Emma for over two years now, and I consider her to be one of the most disturbed children in the school. You've not been here long enough to realise just how much that Emma is lacking in the very thing that every child subconsciously craves. And that is love. I'm not saying that Dr Sinclair doesn't love his daughter, but he is a very busy man and she is left too much in the company of Mrs Rose. An estimable housekeeper and she does her best, but Emma really does need someone younger with her.' He was the third person to make this remark and Helen could not but help feel that they all had a sense of relief because she had come. A great sense of responsibility swept over her and she was hesitant and she answered: 'I realise that Emma still misses her mother, but whether I can help her to overcome what must be a tremendous feeling of abandonment, I don't know.' She looked Neil straight in the face and met his understanding and sympathetic gaze. 'I will try,' she affirmed. She did not tell him of the promising start she had made, seemingly ruined by the arrival on the scene of Maxine Graham.

They talked a little about the routine of the school. Helen discussed with him Emma's love of books and discovered that the girl was very much in advance of the rest of her class when it came to reading.

'Is there a library I can take her to?' asked Helen.

'Yes, there is a very good mobile library that comes every Thursday. It stands in the square from 3–4 so you would just have time to take her after school before you have to be back for evening surgery. It would be a very good idea if you did take her and I am sure it would help her to have a lot of confidence in you. Especially as you obviously share her love of books.'

He was wondering, as he looked at her lovely face, now serious and composed, if she had known all that she was coming to when she accepted the post. As he said good-bye to her, he felt more optimistic at the future prospect for Emma Sinclair than he had ever done.

Helen walked back to Bridge House, quietly going over what Neil had said. She liked him and respected his opinions, and was determined to do her best for Emma, though she could see that this job that she had taken was going to be much more than just the duties of receptionist and secretary. She was not dismayed; she was where she wanted to be and the last thing that was likely to happen was that she would become bored as she might have done in a nine to five job.

That evening she kept her word. She took Emma upstairs and helped her undress, but there were to be no books or television in spite of the entreaty in the child's eyes.

With all the happenings at school she had hardly given a thought to Mark Sinclair and it was with surprise that she found him waiting for her outside his consulting-room when she came downstairs after tucking Emma up. He seemed stiff and his eyes held a hidden anger, but his words were pleasant enough. 'Come into the lounge. Mrs Rose has a log fire going. Would you like a glass of sherry?'

It was the first time she had been in the lovely square room with its moulded ceiling and large fine fireplace in which a cheerful log fire was burning. There were two bookcases and the comfortable armchairs were covered with colourful covers of strong linen. As she sat down she had the strong feeling that the furniture and fabrics of the room had been the doctor's choice and not that of his ex-wife. There was almost a bachelor feel to the room, a certain air of utility, comfort and independence. Helen was silently handed a sherry, Mark taking the chair on the other side of the fireplace.

'Helen,' he began, then hesitated as though trying to make up his mind what to say, 'I won't beat about the bush. I've been talking to Mrs Rose and she tells me that Emma ran away from school again today. Thank you for helping to look for her and taking her back to her class again. Mrs Rose says you were very firm and that it didn't provoke a scene.' He looked worried and concerned as her eyes met his in a searching glance, and Helen groped for words with which to reassure him. 'I've discovered many things about Emma today and I feel that I've got a lot to learn,' she said.

'You've got youth on your side,' he started to say, not knowing that Helen was thinking that it was experience that was needed not youth, and she told him as much, knowing that frank talking was the only way to tackle the problem.

'I know that it should be an advantage, but have you considered taking professional advice?' The immediate stiffening of his face, the closed look that came into his eyes, made her realise that she had said the wrong thing.

'If you mean have I taken her to a psychiatrist the answer is no. I have every respect for the psychiatric profession; in my training it was included in my studies. But no. Emma is my daughter. I understand her. I do understand how she feels and why she has these behaviour problems.' He covered his eyes with his hand. 'I want you to believe that I do love her. I do care deeply that she is not a happy child. I want desperately to put it right, but I can't. I don't know why, but I can't.'

Helen looked at the tortured face and her heart went out to him. Underneath the severe exterior, he had suddenly chosen to show her an inner feeling that no one would have believed to have existed. Again that overwhelming sense of responsibility swept over her. She had felt it that afternoon. But could she do for Emma what they had all failed to do? Here now was her father surely about to make the same demands upon her.

Mark looked up, the desperate appeal in his eyes softened his expression. Involuntarily her hand went towards him, and she found it grasped in both of his. The contact, so unexpected, and in an atmosphere charged with emotion sent shivers of feeling coursing through her. She did not know it, but her face, as Mark looked at her, was soft with sympathy, her eyes bright with unshed tears and her mouth tremulous.

He was moved to say gently to her, 'Can you help me, Helen?' He was still holding her hands and did not let them go, willing her to give the answer he so much wanted to hear.

She looked into his eyes 'I promise I will. I don't know what I can do, but I will try, I will.'

He pressed her hands tightly in a simple gesture of gratitude. As he got up, and stood near the fire looking down at her, a faint smile came into his eyes and his hand went out and for one instant lay caressingly on the top of her soft hair. 'I am thinking that it was a good day when you came to Bridge House.' His arm dropped round her shoulder and lay there as though deriving comfort. He moved towards the door.

'I must go and do some writing up now. Goodnight and thank you.'

Helen was left staring into the flames. She was more shaken than she dared to admit by his words and his touch. He had said it was a good day when she came here; somewhere in the bottom of her heart she was hoping it was too.

# CHAPTER THREE

Next morning Helen woke to find herself happily looking forward to a full day in the surgery. She would meet Dr Wharton for the first time on one of his two morning surgeries of the week. Many of his patients had been with him for years and were all eager to introduce themselves to the new receptionist. Helen liked their blunt and pleasant welcome.

Mark had brought Dr Wharton into the waiting-room before anyone had arrived and made the introductions. The younger doctor's manner was courteous and rather distant, contrasting strongly with the emotional outburst of the night before. Helen looked at him expecting an answering look of friendliness. She did not receive it and felt snubbed. She shook hands with Dr Wharton thinking all the time of Mark—was he feeling embarrassed after their conversation?—but she found she had no time to think about such things as she had to answer the older doctor's greeting.

'I'm going to call you Helen. I've heard about you already from young Emma. You must have made an impression there; as I came in she was on her way to school and couldn't wait to tell me that her Daddy had got a new "lady".' He looked keenly at Helen. 'I gather she ran off again yesterday. She needs a stabilising influence in her life, and now that I've met you, I can only say that I hope you've come for a good long time.' His eyes twinkled at her and she felt her colour rising. He laughed and said, 'Don't let an old man's teasing upset you. I've had Mark with me a number of years now, long enough to know that he desperately needs someone to help him with Emma.' He patted her shoulder. 'I'm off to my room now. You know where to find me should you need any help.'

Helen looked after his sturdy figure and white head disappearing into his consulting-room. Yet another who was relying on her to be able to manage Emma. She hoped she wasn't going to let them all down.

The morning was busy with two lots of patients to see to. Sheila popped in to ask how she was getting on and to have a word with Dr Wharton, whom she treated like a favourite uncle.

'He's a darling,' she said to Helen. 'The younger patients prefer to see Mark, yet Dr Wharton is very good with children, and he loves Emma.' She helped Helen tidy the magazines, and Helen enjoyed the chat and the chance to ask Sheila about one or two of the patients.

At lunch-time Mrs Rose and Helen were joined by Mark, who was having a quick break before he went off on his visits. Helen felt that there was a slight restraint between them still. He chatted about things in general, asking her how she was getting on in the waiting-room. She told him of Sheila's help and how much she was enjoying the curiosity and friendly spirit of the people of Hexton.

'It's not like a big London surgery,' she remarked, 'where there are three or four receptionists in a separate room and the waiting-room consists of a gloomy circle of people, none of them talking to the other. Here, because I'm in the same room everyone has a word of greeting, and then they all settle down to talk to one another. They really are friendly and nice.' She smiled across the table at Mark but received no response.

He looked at her steadily as though his thoughts were elsewhere.

'Yorkshire people are friendly and nice,' he repeated, 'and the longer you know them the nicer they are.' And with these words he got up from the table and went on his way. Helen had soon learned that the practice covered a very wide area around Hexton. There were small villages further up the dale and a call often had to be made to one of the more remote farms on the fell side. The Range Rover was a very necessary vehicle on some of the steep tracks, especially in winter weather.

The day was to be a settling in one; Helen managed the afternoon surgery on her own after meeting Emma from school. That young lady seemed to be quite pleased to see her and after tea Emma was proud to show Helen all her books. She was delighted when Helen told her about the Mobile Library and by bed-time Helen felt they had made some progress towards getting to know one another and establishing a firm and trusting relationship.

Her first week passed very quickly, she spent an hour each evening with Emma and they now had a happy routine of books and favourite games. Mark was cool but pleasant when they met after surgery or at meal-times; a reserve seemed to have come over him and she wondered if ever again she would see the real Mark who had given her a brief glimpse of his inner torment, during their first evening at the beginning of the week. On Sunday she woke to her first day off, and as she looked up the dale from her bedroom window she could see that the day promised to be fine. It was now well into March and although it could be a treacherous month, some days seemed to hold a promise of spring and a slightly milder feeling in the air after the rigours of winter. Today was such a day and she wondered what she would do with it. She was tempted to walk up on to the moor, but decided once again to take the car over into Wedderdale.

She spent a wonderful morning, parking the car on the crest of the moor before the road dipped down into the next dale. As she walked along the track, she felt an exhilaration she had not experienced for a long time; the wind whipped sharp and cold about her ears but all that was forgotten when she gazed at the view that opened out before her. Garthdale was behind her and opening out in front was the whole of Wedderdale; and beyond and beyond again in the clear air the hills revealed their soft contours in blues and greys. 'It's like being on top of the world,' she thought happy and excited at finding herself in such a lovely place. She left the car and took the track along the ridge, broad and stony, but easy walking and affording her the chance to take in the glorious views on all sides. She had a sense of coming home, of belonging, and all the despair she had felt in London had gone, replaced by a sense of wonder and contentment.

She had lunch in Hesketh and spent the afternoon exploring Wedderdale. On her way back she could not resist stopping once again at the track that divided the two dales, and she had a last quick walk in the early evening air.

When she arrived back at Bridge House, Mark and Mrs Rose were in the kitchen. She did not know that her face glowed with health and exercise, her hair blown by the wind, making her look younger than her years. She was eager to tell them where she had been and was smiling as she looked at Mark. Her look brought no answering response from him and she felt her excitement falter. Little did she realise that he had been given a sharp and bitter reminder of what had been. Of a young wife, also vital and beautiful, in whom the love and enthusiasm of early marriage had turned to disillusion; and who, unlike the smiling girl before him, had hated the very hills, the very places that were bringing happiness to Helen. He watched her go upstairs, his eyes thoughtful and full of internal conflict. He remembered her kindness and sympathy on the day Emma had run away from school, but this remembrance was clouded by the words that Maxine had used to him the previous evening when they had met for dinner. He had known Maxine for over a year and had come to value her companionship and her judgement. What was the truth of Maxine's insinuations? Helen had been here only a very short time. To his knowledge, Maxine had met her only twice, but he knew his friend to be shrewd and intelligent, he could not believe that she might be deliberately malicious. But her words regarding Helen had remained strongly in his memory.

'She seems to be getting on well with Emma.' Maxine had remarked and he had agreed with her, but then had come the warning rejoinder.

'If you are not careful she will be turning her girlish sweetness on you too. I know the kind. She will do anything for Emma just to gain your approval. She will end up by embarrassing you with a lovelorn devotion.

Emma will only suffer by it.' As he started to protest the older woman looked at him intently and seriously. 'It's not for me to advise you, but I think it would be in your best interests if you keep a businesslike relationship with her.'

Maxine had spoken calmly and he had no reason to doubt the sincerity of her words. He had known unmarried colleagues in the past who had found difficulty in keeping the close relationship of a doctor and young receptionist from becoming too intimate. He agreed with Maxine and knew that caution was necessary, but these admissions did not stop him from seeing the candid sympathy of Helen's eyes and feeling again the clasp of her hand in his. He shook his head slowly. Maxine was right, he would be careful what he confided to Helen, but at the same time he was not going to be deterred from fostering the growing friendship between Helen and Emma.

Not knowing that she was the subject of Mark's speculation, Helen settled down to a quiet evening in her room. She had had an enjoyable day and faced her second week at Bridge House with confidence and pleasure. London, Sadlers and above all, Jeremy, seemed to be a different world, a lifetime away. She had no time to think of her heartache, it was all behind her and she had the strongest, inescapable feeling that she had done the right thing in coming to Yorkshire.

On her next afternoon off she had not decided what to do and was sitting over lunch talking to Mrs Rose and Mark. He suddenly asked her if she had yet found her way up Garthdale. She shook her head and told him that on both of her previous excursions she had gone in the Wedderdale direction.

'I'm glad to know that you are getting to know the area,' he said, 'because I have a favour to ask you.'

Helen was surprised and looked at him enquiringly.

'I know it's your afternoon off,' he explained, 'but I wondered if you would like the chance to get to know another part of the dale. Jim Kirby, up at Oxhope Farm, beyond Smurthwaite, needs some tablets and is too busy with lambing to come down to Hexton. I thought you might like a trip up there this afternoon. Emma loves going to the Kirbys' farm and I believe they have some sheepdog puppies that she would like to see. You could meet her from school and take her with you.' He ended on a half question, but Helen had no hesitation.

'I'd love to go,' she said 'It's straight up the dale beyond Keldbeck isn't it? I will soon find the way.'

'Good.' He sounded quite pleased. 'I'll have the tablets ready for you before you go to pick up Emma.'

Helen spent the early part of the afternoon

studying the map of the part she was to visit. She heard the doctor return from his visits and later called out on an emergency, but she did not see him again before taking the Mini round to the school and parking it outside to wait for Emma.

The children soon started to appear, the older ones to make their own way home, while the mothers, smiling and chatting to each other, met the younger children. It seemed to Helen as though about half the children climbed into the bus that was waiting. Like the doctors' practice the school served a large area and the children came from all the villages further up the dale that were too small to have their own school. Some of the youngsters would be taken to the lane leading up to an isolated farm; there they would be met by their father or mother in the Landrover that was the universal vehicle of the dale farmer.

Helen was just beginning to wonder what had happened to Emma when she appeared with Jane Elstow. Helen walked into the playground while Emma ran to meet her; already there was a change in the difficult child of the previous week and the look and smile exchanged with Helen and the teacher seemed to acknowledge it.

'Why have you brought the car?' Emma asked. 'Are we going somewhere?'

Helen put her arm round the child's shoulders and gave her a little hug.

'I've got a treat for you. You go and sit in the car and I will come and tell you all about it.'

Emma ran off, leaving Helen and Jane to walk slowly over the playground and giving Helen a chance to ask if Emma had been any better. Jane gave a pleased reply: 'I wouldn't have believed it would have made so much difference so quickly,' she said. 'She has found a friend: she trusts you. Before she was alone in that big house with Mrs Rose and a father who was seldom there. Mrs Rose is very kind but you could not expect someone of her age to cope with tantrums and sulks. It wasn't a question of her not caring for Emma, but there's a lot of difference between caring and understanding. And that's what's happened, since you've been here. You have entered into Emma's world and to her it's like a light coming into her life.'

Helen interrupted 'But I've not really done anything. It's only been a short time, I've hardly had a chance.'

'I know, but she has mentioned to me one or two small things that made me realise that you had managed to break down that prickly armour she used to present to everybody.' Jane continued: 'You have offered to take her to the mobile library to let her choose some books. No one has even bothered to think of whether she had enough books before. She loves reading. I know I've said it before, but to an only child it's usually a very important thing. The books take them into a world they can't experience because they do not have the usual play contact of brothers and sisters. I'm not for a moment saying that reading is a substitute for having other children around you, but I've found that with only children it's very important.'

'It seemed such a little thing,' said Helen thoughtfully. 'But I suppose it must have opened a door to her. I'm going to take her up the dale to one of the farms now. Dr Sinclair says there are some sheepdog puppies there and she will love that.'

They had reached the car and said goodbye, with the mutual suggestion that perhaps they could meet one evening or at the weekend. Jane had rooms above a shop in Hexton and Helen was pleased to think that there was someone she could meet when she wasn't working.

She found Emma in the car.

'Where are we going?' asked the child, her little face full of shining eagerness.

'To Mr Kirby's at Oxhope to take him some tablets.'

Nothing could have pleased Emma more. 'I like it there,' she said 'He has three sheepdogs.'

'I think they will be out with Mr Kirby as he is still lambing, but your Daddy says there are some puppies we can see.'

A wistful look replaced the eager one. 'I wish I could have one.'

Helen looked at her. 'Would you like a dog?' Emma nodded and Helen asked her: 'Have you never had one?'

'No,' said Emma sadly. 'Mummy wouldn't have one, and then there was no one to look after a dog, so I never asked again.'

'Well, I'm not making any promises because I don't know what your Daddy thinks about it, but perhaps one day when I have been here a bit longer I will ask him.'

'Are you going to stay, Helen? I like it better now that you are here and not just that horrid Maxine.'

Helen had not liked Maxine either and sympathised with Emma but, putting the key into the car and starting up the engine, she felt she should make a suitable reply. 'Mrs Graham is a good friend of your father's and I don't think he would be very pleased to hear you talking like that.' And changing the subject quickly, she said: 'Now, do you know the way to Oxhope? I've not been there before so you will have to help me.'

The diversion worked and Emma was soon chatting away and pointing out landmarks on the narrow road that followed the River Garth up the dale. Helen needed all her attention for the bends and twists that wound down to the village of Keldbeck. It was a typical dales village, straddling the river, houses and cottages rising steeply from the bridge. The weathered stone walls and roofs, that had been there for hundreds of years, nestled into the shelter of the hillside. Only one road went through Keldbeck and the signpost said Smurthwaite 3, Garth Head 4. After that the way followed the ancient track over the moor and down into Linton Bridge, a village in neighbouring Wedderdale.

Smurthwaite was not more than a collection of cottages with a small chapel, and they were soon through it and looking for the turning to Oxhope. Helen found it with Emma's help, but was not prepared for the steep gradient as the farm road left the valley. The Mini coped very well and they climbed steadily up the walled lane to the farm, the last part of the journey being a stony track over the fields bringing them to the old, low farmhouse. Emma immediately ran up to the front door but Helen stopped to look at the view across to the other side of the dale. She was looking at identical small farms, settled into the hillside for centuries, each with its patchwork of grey stone walls. The green of the fields soon gave way above to the rough brown of the moor— space, permanence, and what must be a struggle for living in such a remote area, where sheep farming is the only means of survival. Helen turned away from the lovely scene and followed Emma into the farmhouse. A short, smiling woman greeted her at the door.

'Emma tells me you've brought Jim's tablets. I'm ever so grateful to you, Miss er . . . Doctor did tell me your name but I've gone and forgot it.'

'I think Helen will do.' She shook hands with the farmer's wife. 'I'm pleased to meet you, Mrs Kirby. It's the first time I've been up the dale. You've got a lovely view.'

'Yes, I suppose it's nice, but views don't count for much when the winter drags on and the lambing's late. It's hard for Jim and him not getting any younger. But I mustn't be grumbling when you've come all this way. Be coming in and I'll get some tea on. Then I know Emma will want to see the pups.'

Helen looked round the small warm kitchen, a fire roaring in the grate, pictures of Mrs Kirby's family, wedding photographs, school pictures of her grandchildren on the mantelpiece. Like the kitchen at Bridge House it had a modern fridge, cooker and washer, but the small window and the thick walls gave to it the solid feeling of a room which had served generations of the family through many hard winters. Again she experienced the sense of permanence and unchanging continuity that she had felt when she was outside looking over the other side of the dale.

The hot tea and freshly baked scones and fruit cake were very welcome and Emma seemed to be a different child, chattering away to Mrs Kirby and asking her about the puppies.

'They'll soon be ready to go to their new homes,' said Mrs Kirby. 'It's a good job you came today. Another week and they'd be gone.'

'Are they all going to farms to be trained as sheepdogs?' asked Helen.

'Oh yes,' was the reply. 'We've always bred from our Trixie. She's a good mother and very intelligent the pups are. Soon learn they do, if they get with a farmer who's used to trainin'. Would you like to go and see them now, Emma? I should put your coat on again; it's cold out in the barn. Always a cold wind up here there is.'

Emma didn't have to be asked twice and the three of them went out to the old stone barn which stood adjoining the house. Yelps and shrieks soon filled the air. The black dogs with their patches of white and their soft new coats were tumbling all over with playfulness. Emma had no fear of the dogs and rolled them over to be stroked and patted. Helen watched her happy face, and made up her mind, that as soon as she had the opportunity she would ask Mark if they could have a puppy for Emma.

It was a hard job persuading Emma to leave the puppies but it was soon time to be getting back to Bridge House where Mrs Rose would have their tea waiting for them. They stood by the Mini and said good-bye to Mrs Kirby, promising to come again soon. Emma sat strapped in the back seat and Helen started the engine. She could not believe it when it spluttered and stopped. She tried again and again but it was completely dead.

'Won't it start?' a thin little voice said, from the back of the car.

'No, it won't,' snapped Helen. 'You'd better go back to Mrs Kirby.' The farmer's wife was waiting at the farm door, a worried look on her face.

'Sounds as though as the battery's flat and Jim right up on the moor. Whatever can we do?'

Helen sat down abruptly on the kitchen chair, Emma held her hand.

'Shall we ask Daddy to come?' she said tentatively. Helen frowned; she had never felt so useless, but the last thing she wanted to do was to ring up and admit her failure to Mark. But if it was the battery the best thing would be for him to bring the Range Rover up to the farm to get the Mini started. A sick knawing gripped her stomach. She looked down at the small girl and across to Mrs Kirby.

'Doctor'll come and get you started. Do you want to phone him?' The two of them seemed to be making the decision for her. Reluctantly she went to the phone in the sitting room and dialled Bridge House. Mrs Rose fetched Mark to the phone, she hardly recognised his voice as he uttered a terse greeting. Haltingly she explained what had happened and was not prepared for his angry, short reaction.

'Aren't you even capable of taking a car ten miles up the dale? Stay where you are. I suppose I'd better come.' The phone was slammed down and Helen was left trembling with the unexpected harshness of his words.

Emma came into the room. 'Was Daddy cross?' she whispered. 'Sometimes he gets cross if he's been up all night with a patient.'

Helen looked at her. There were times when the child seemed to have an understanding beyond her years, resulting she supposed from living with adults in a busy doctors' practice. Still smarting from the unjust criticism of the words she had heard over the phone, she tried to pull herself together for Emma's sake. They joined Mrs Kirby in the kitchen where the kind woman had made tea for them. Helen tried to make her voice sound light, despite the hollow sickness she felt.

'Dr Sinclair is coming up straight away. I'm sorry, Mrs Kirby, for causing you so much trouble. It's only the third time I've had the Mini out, I suppose I'm not used to it yet.'

They drank their tea and Mrs Kirby kept Emma interested by showing her the old wooden box of toys she had in the kitchen for her grandchildren when they came to visit her. Emma soon got absorbed in a jig-saw, leaving Helen and Mrs Kirby to chat about life on an isolated hill farm. If Helen had not felt so worried about Mark's imminent arrival she would have been fascinated to hear about a life so different to any she had ever known.

A sudden roar of an engine on the steep track to the farm announced the doctor's arrival, and they all rushed to the front door. Helen went up to Mark and started to apologise as he got out of the Range Rover, but not even looking at her he brushed past and went over to the Mini. His tall figure seemed to bend double as he lowered himself into the small car. The next moment the unbelievable sound of a purring engine filled the air. Dumbfounded Helen went up to the car as Mark got out and stood looking at her. He saw the anxious, bewildered face and her dark hair blowing in the wind, he heard her faltering, protesting tones. His impatience, his strained tired eyes ignored her straight appealing look and he remembered only the words of warning that Maxine had used at the weekend.

'It's quite obvious,' his voice was clipped, 'that you used too much choke and flooded the engine; if you'd just left the car for half-an-hour and tried again it would have started easily. There was no need to put on a little-girl-lost act and call me all the way up here to no purpose.'

He strode back to his own car and roared off leaving a speechless Helen returning to the farmhouse to Mrs Kirby and Emma. His words went round and round in her head; he had treated her like a child, making no allowance for the fact that the car was strange to her and it was the first time she had driven in such steep, rough country. Fury and indignation seethed inside her; to think she had felt sorry for him, he was hateful, unbearable. Hardly knowing what she was saying, she told Emma to get into the car and said goodbye to Mrs Kirby. She did not speak to Emma all the way back to Bridge House, the car seemed to negotiate the narrow lanes of its own volition. She parked the car in the drive and Emma ran in to Mrs Rose. Knowing that the little girl would soon be relating the whole of the episode to the housekeeper, Helen ran upstairs to her room, collapsed into the chair where she stayed for a long, long time trying to sort out her jumbled emotions. Trying to sort out the enigma that was Mark Sinclair. In just two weeks she had seen so many sides to the man who was her employer. She had liked and respected the quiet courtesy and friendliness he had shown her at the interview; she knew he was beloved by his patients up and down the dale; he had given her a glimpse of the vulnerable human being underneath the businesslike exterior and she had extended her sympathy and felt she would come to like him. Then the softness and honesty had retreated as though he had regretted the confidences he had reposed in her and she had become accustomed to the cool politeness of his everyday contact with her. Now this: impatience, rage and dislike all boiling over into what seemed to her an intolerable and inexplicable misjudgement. Would she ever get to know him; did she even want to? Unanswerable questions, and she stirred herself at last, and made a drink before going to put Emma to bed, little knowing that before the night was out she was to see yet another side of the complex character of the man who had come to the forefront of her life.

She had said goodnight to Emma and was just settling in her room when she heard a quiet tentative knock on the door. Puzzled, she got up and opened the door. To her utter astonishment it was Mark standing there. Uncomfortable, diffident was the expression in his eyes, a long way from the anger of the afternoon. She was stunned into silence, and as her eyes met his she knew he must sense the resentment she felt towards him.

'Helen.' He spoke her name softly. 'I know that I am risking a rebuff, but I have come to ask you if you will let me take you out for an hour.' He must have noticed that her whole body stiffened in antagonism and refusal, for he continued quietly: 'Don't say no, please come and give me a chance to explain what happened this afternoon.'

He didn't smile but his voice was persuasively low and against her will she found herself silently nodding agreement. A half smile came from him then, and as he turned away he said, 'Put on a warm coat and something for your head, and I'll be waiting down at the car.'

She turned involuntarily to find her coat, thinking to herself that she must be crazy. One minute hating the man, the next agreeing to go out with him. What was his attraction, his magnetism, what was it in his words and manner that could turn her from stubborn resentment to submission at a glance? She shook her coat on, found a woollen head-square and ran down the stairs feeling in herself an eagerness that could not be denied.

She slid quietly into the car not saying a word, and after a nod of approval but no comment Mark started the engine and turned out of Bridge House into the square, now deserted but cheerfully lit. At the church they took a road that Helen had not been along before, though she knew it led to the moor above Hexton that she had looked on when she had stopped on the way to Wedderdale. Once out of the small town it became narrower than most of the country lanes that Helen had been along, there seemed to be just enough room for the Range Rover between the walls so close on either side. Mark drove slowly and carefully, though at this time of the evening, thought Helen, you would hardly expect to meet any other vehicles. The road twisted and climbed but still no word was spoken; Helen felt a tension between them, not being quite able to sense his mood. Suddenly the walls stopped and the moor opened up before them, the headlights picking out a narrow bridge where a ghyll ran down to join the main river. Mark stopped the car on the short grass at the side of the bridge, and leaned in front of her to open her door. The cold night air met her and she shivered as she stepped out and walked round to the front of the car to join Mark. The darkness hid the expression on his face but his voice showed an uncharacteristic kindly concern.

'You're cold,' he murmured, and to her astonishment slipped an arm round her shoulders drawing her close. She did not realise how much resistance she showed until his next words.

'Still hating me? Come and see why I've brought you here and then I'll try to make amends.' Still holding her close he guided her to the other side of the bridge and they leaned over the parapet; there was not much water in the ghyll, but the soft trickle over the stones sounded clear in the still night air.

All Mark had to say, was 'There you are!' and there was pride in his voice, as well as warmth and affection. Helen was looking across the dale. It was a dark but starry night; on the far slopes glinted a myriad of lights which could only be the little market town. She thought of the families she had already got to know; she looked further up the dale and here and there an isolated glimmer showed the presence of the dales people in their sturdy farmhouses. The lights seemed to spell out a secure, community feeling which you could only find in remoter country areas such as this. Then she heard Mark's voice, musing almost as though she was not there. 'This is where I come after a difficult day. It's dark and it's cold but there in front of me, with peace all around me, I can imagine my people safe in their homes . . .' He stopped. 'Do you think I am foolish, Helen?'

She looked at the little township nestled in front of her, at the same time remembering the faces of anxious or ill patients in the surgery, the children being brought for injections, the pregnant mums at the ante-natal clinic. They were his people and his feelings revealed how deeply he loved the community medicine he practiced.

'No,' she replied slowly, 'I think I can understand, even though I've been here such a short time. There's sense of belonging in a small country town like Hexton, and whether you are the local doctor, the headmaster, or just the doctor's receptionist you somehow become part of it all, and every single aspect of local life matters to you—even the bright lights from their homes on a winter's night.'

He listened to her words and experienced a

feeling of one-ness he had not felt for a long time. His mind drifted into the past and into sadness, but he would not let that mood overcome this feeling of sharing on the dark hillside. His next words were in lighter vein. 'Can you pick out Bridge House?' he asked her. 'If you look hard you can find the square, and I've often tried to find the house but I'm never quite sure.'

Helen's gaze followed his pointing arm, and she looked closely at the cluster of lights. 'Yes,' she said, 'You can see the square, the lighting is brighter and where the lights finish must be the line of the river by the bridge; so those must be Riverside Cottages and the next patch of lights must be Bridge House.'

Her delight was almost childlike and for a moment he tightened his arm round her shoulders. As he did so Maxine's voice came unbidden to his mind, but surely she must be wrong. He could detect no deviousness in Helen, nothing but a straightforward honesty and simplicity which he couldn't help liking. A momentary frown came into his face as he envisaged bringing Maxine to this spot. He had never done it, knowing that her presence there would be accompanied by impatience and ridicule and that his solitary oasis of the dark evenings would be ruined for ever. And yet he had brought this girl here, knowing deep within him what her reaction would be and he was not disappointed. His deep sigh made

Helen turn her face up towards him and for one moment he rested his lips gently on her forehead, not in a kiss, but in an acknowledgement that this moment was right and he wanted her to know it. A shiver shook her small frame, whether of cold or emotion he did not know. His cheek resting against her head, he whispered, 'I'm a brute to keep you out here; we can sit in the car and still admire the view.'

She did not protest and they were soon in the warmth and comfort of the car, the view was the same but their mood had subtly changed. Helen felt closer to Mark than she had ever done, but at the back of her mind was the scene of the afternoon and she felt unable to say anything to match the easy comradeship that had existed outside on the bridge. Mark must have read her thoughts as he suddenly leant on the steering wheel keeping his gaze straight ahead and not meeting her eyes. She had not expected an apology and when it came she felt surprise and remorse. Surprise that the grim, autocratic person of the afternoon was unexpectedly contrite, and remorse that her own fury and resentment had shown itself so patently at the time of the incident.

'Helen,' he said and she turned her head towards him, 'I'm sorry I lost my temper this afternoon. I'm afraid your telephone call was the last straw in a series of trying events. I shouldn't make excuses for myself but I was up half the night with a difficult birth, as you know the morning surgery was hectic, then straight after I'd finished my visits there was an emergency call to an accident on the Leeds road. I'd just got back to the house when your call came. I wasn't very pleasant to you, was I?'

Helen hardly knew how to reply; his words were so unexpected and undramatic, that they left her feeling that she was the one who had been in the wrong. 'I didn't know.' She was the apologetic one now. 'I felt awful about the Mini and you were the only person I knew to turn to. Emma said she thought you had been up in the night—she seems to understand a lot for her age, doesn't she?'

Somehow the name of Emma seemed to have bridged an awkward gap between them. They talked about her for a few minutes and Helen was pleased that Mark already seemed to sense that there was a change in her.

'She seems happier,' he remarked. 'She hasn't run away from school since your first day and the sulky little child who hardly ever spoke seems to have vanished. I think I have you to thank for that, Helen.' He looked at the girl's profile in the dim light. She was serious and the genuine concern she was feeling for Emma showed itself clearly in her intent pose and gaze. 'What are you thinking about?' he asked. She turned to him with a smile that was so candid and direct that it caught at his heart.

'I expect it will surprise you as it's a very

down to earth request. I promised Emma that I would ask you if she could have a puppy. She loved seeing the sheepdog pups this afternoon and I think a dog is a good companion for an only child. It would give her something to think about apart from herself. But she gave me the idea that she had asked before and that you had said no. But I do think it would be a good thing and I would help. Please would you consider it?'

All his former friendliness seemed to vanish and Helen felt a sense of shock at his next words.

'No,' he said shortly. 'I don't want her to have a dog. Maxine doesn't like dogs.'

In the total silence that followed, there seemed nothing for Helen to say and as though that was the end of the conversation, he turned the key and started up the engine. In a few moments, they were off the moor and on their way back to Hexton, the spell broken.

As they drew into Bridge House and stopped, Helen felt she had to say something. 'Thank you very much for taking me out. I enjoyed it.' Her polite words seemed to irritate him and he leaned towards her placing his hands on her shoulders. Roughly he drew her to him and his lips claimed hers in a deep, rough kiss that caused her to struggle away from him. Her action served only to inflame his passion and as the kiss deepened, Helen felt the struggle lessen and an intense desire to return his seeking embrace, swept over her. As his lips moved and found her neck she gave a shiver of desire and delight and her arms of their own volition twined around him and drew him closer; his hand slipped inside her coat caressing her and finding her breast. A trembling shock of heady sensation sent her mind reeling backwards; she was in the past engulfed in a passion that frightened her. She tore herself from his lips, from his grasp, fumbled with the car door and rushed up the steps of Bridge House, until the next thing she knew was that she was lying panting and sobbing on her bed. The conflicting emotions of the day had been too much for her—she had seen everything from Mark—friendliness, anger, contempt, contrition, tenderness and at the last, passion. A passion that she wanted to return but dare not; still so deep was the feeling that passion could only be given where there was love. She wearily and confusedly drifted into sleep with a hazy and sorrowful conviction that Mark could not give her that love even if she wanted it.

## CHAPTER FOUR

Helen awoke the following morning after a night of tossing and turning; her dreams a nightmare mixture of Mark, the almost forgotten and far-distant Jeremy, and the old difficult Emma screaming because she couldn't have a puppy.

She lay awake for a while wondering how she was going to summon up the courage to face Mark after the events of the evening before.

A happy chattering Emma helped her through breakfast-time and she did not see Mark before he appeared in the waiting-room while she was sitting at the desk sorting out the morning's notes. It was with relief that she looked up, and saw his face with its old reserve; he said little, took the notes and disappeared into the consulting room. He had set the tone of their relationship and she was glad to follow his lead. She was kept busy all the morning and he went on his rounds without stopping for lunch. She had an illogical feeling of relief that was combined with a sense of losing something from her life. After lunch she settled down to her typing and it was soon time to meet Emma from school.

She had got to know several of the mothers waiting each day outside the school and was glad to make pleasant and normal conversation about children's ailments and behaviour. Emma came running happily across the playground closely followed by Neil Brandon. She shouted to Helen, 'I told Mr Brandon about the puppies, Helen. Am I going to have one? Did you ask Daddy?'

Helen thought that a white lie was the only

way out and called herself a coward. 'He says no at the moment, Emma, but perhaps we will ask him again when the weather gets better.'

Neil patted the small girl on the head. 'I think summer is the best time to have a puppy don't you?'

This was making matters worse and Helen hastily changed the subject, asking what date the school went back after the Easter holiday which was getting near.

Neil walked with them to the car and detained Helen while Emma climbed into the back. 'Talking about Easter,' he said to Helen, 'there's an Alan Ayckbourn play on at Leeds and I wondered if you would like to go and see it with me?'

Helen's look was one of surprise and gratification. The only thing she had missed since she had left London were the evenings at the theatre and here was a heaven-sent opportunity to think of something that had no connection with Mark.

'Thank you, Neil. I'd love to go. I've missed not going to the theatre.' Neil's smile was all she needed to tell her she had pleased him, and by the time she got into the car, they had fixed up the visit to Leeds and she had arranged to spend the following Sunday with him. She was not able to resist the offer of being taken over to Wharfedale, have lunch out, and if the weather was fine to go walking at Kettlewell.

She got back to the 4.30 surgery feeling that she could face Mark more easily; what she was not prepared for was to find Maxine in the waiting-room, or for her opening words. 'I saw you talking to Neil Brandon at the school. You seem to be on very friendly terms with him. He's an extremely nice young man and I hope he's offered to take you out.'

Helen's stammered reply was cut short by the terse voice of Mark standing in the door behind her. 'Miss Wainwright has to prepare for evening surgery now, Maxine. Come into my room for a moment and we'll make our arrangements for this evening.'

Helen stood by her desk as Maxine walked out of the waiting-room. There seemed to be triumph in her step and the toss of her head. The only thought in Helen's head was how could you possibly dislike a person so much when you hardly knew her? She was thankful when the first patients arrived and her attention and her time were taken up.

During the next few weeks, Helen found it hard to believe that the incident with Mark on the dark hillside and later in the car had ever happened. She saw him every day before surgery and often at lunch-time but his attitude could only be described as distant and polite. Often in the evenings she heard Maxine's voice for a few moments before the couple drove off to spend the evening together.

Her thoughts and undiscovered feelings she put firmly into the background and as time went on and the cold late winter blossomed into spring, her life became even and pleasant.

She had struck up a firm friendship with Jane Elstow; the girls were the same age and both living away from home, though Jane was a Yorkshire girl, her parents living at Malton not far from York. Helen would often spend the evening in Jane's small flat; they both preferred a quiet evening chatting or watching television than going into Leeds, as was the custom with many of the young people of Hexton. Jane had no car, and occasionally on a Saturday afternoon they would take the Mini to go shopping in Harrogate or York. Jane had no boy-friend and Helen sometimes wondered if her friend had a hidden and unspoken liking for Neil. However the impression may have been suggested simply because of Jane's regard for Neil as her head-teacher. At school they were in constant contact with one another and it was obvious that Neil held Jane high in his estimation as a teacher.

Neil was the other reason for Helen's contentment. He had fulfilled his promise to take her out on Sundays when Emma was usually off with her father and Maxine. These trips no longer seemed to upset the little girl who caused no more trouble that term. Helen found that she looked forward to the hour after tea that she spent with Emma. This time

86

was usually spent in Helen's room where Emma loved to be; the shadow of her mother's presence was fading, with the young company that Helen was able to give. As the evenings got lighter towards the end of the Easter holidays, the pair took to taking walks along the river and up the hillside. Early spring flowers were appearing, the trees wore their first coat of green and Emma seemed to delight in being out in the fresh air, running off the energy that had stored up after a term at school. These days she never seemed to stop chattering and when Helen stopped to think she realised what a change there was in the small child. These observations were tinged with regret that Mark did not seem to want to share in his daughter's young life. He saw her only at meal times and then he was teasing and cheerful with her, but Helen could see no close bond between the two of them.

Helen tried to make up for Mark's lack of affection and did not find this difficult; she had become very fond of Emma and went out of her way to give her the love that had been so long lacking in her life. By the end of the holidays she was helped in this by Neil who sometimes joined them for their evening walk or exploration. If Mark disapproved no word or remark was said. His work filled his life and what time he had to spare he seemed content to spend in Maxine's company.

Helen would have had a surprise had she

been able to eavesdrop on one of Mark and Maxine's conversations one evening. As usual they were having coffee after dinner in Maxine's spacious and comfortable lounge above the gallery. Maxine's taste was excellent, and the room, while being too much on the spare modern style for Mark's comfort, was furnished with beautiful contemporary print chairs, the bare walls hung with just one or two original oils, painted by Ben Morland, one of Maxine's friends who exhibited at the gallery. While Mark could not deny the excellence and unique workmanship of the paintings, the harsh colours and angular aspects were not to his liking and he did not find the works of art conducive to relaxation.

Maxine herself was relaxed and happy; she always was in Mark's company. She had known him a long time and while their interests were dissimilar they each seemed to be able to give to the other a companionship that was satisfying to both of them though one subject always provoked disagreement between them, and that was Emma. Maxine, a divorcée with no children, was a hard-headed business woman, and had no liking for the child. Although she tried to hide her dislike to stay in Mark's favour, there were times when her opinions contrasted sharply with those of the child's father. But it was not the subject of Emma tonight that set off words of discord between them. It was Helen. Regarding Mark as her property, Maxine saw Helen as a threat and her thinly-veiled comments were designed to steer Mark's thoughts in her direction and not towards that of his receptionist. She had noted with pleasure the growing friendship between Helen and Neil and sought the ideal moment to make capital out of it.

Mark was relaxed and content, even if not happy. Maxine knew his moods and tolerated his tiredness at the end of his busy day. He was reflecting that life had become easier since Helen had come into the practice and had achieved such good progress with Emma, and he told Maxine so.

Maxine gave him a penetrating glance. 'I think you have Neil Brandon to thank for some of that,' she said quietly. Mark's head came up with a jerk. 'Neil?' he answered sharply. 'I know that he takes Helen out from time to time but the relationship seems very casual and friendly. I don't sense any romance there.'

Maxine laughed 'Oh Mark, you are naive sometimes. Can't you see that Neil worships the ground that Helen walks on? There will be wedding bells there soon, you see. Then we will have to do something about Emma.' There was no laughter in Mark's eyes, at Maxine's words. A picture had come to him of a slim dark-haired girl standing defiantly holding Emma's hand at Oxhope Farm. A kaleidoscope of pictures and thoughts followed. He had got so used to her sitting quietly and efficiently behind the desk in the waiting room; then he remembered his feelings on the evening she had so loved seeing the lights of Hexton from the hillside; his thoughts faltered as he also recalled the sequel to this when she had at first seemed to return his kisses, but suddenly had shrunk from him and run off into the darkness. He knew since then there had been a coolness between them, and neither had he failed to notice how frequently Neil Brandon's car was to be found parked outside Bridge House. Was Maxine right? He knew her to be shrewd and observant; but why this sudden sinking in the pit of his stomach at the thought of losing Helen? The thought occurred too that Emma would once again become the problem he had failed so miserably to tackle.

'Mark, dear.' Maxine's softly spoken words brought him back to his present surroundings, and he listened to her repeating what he had only half-heard the first time. 'Did you hear what I said? If Helen marries Neil, we shall have to think seriously about Emma. We can't go back to the situation as it was before, the constant running away from school, her general intractable behaviour. Don't you think it is about time to be thinking of sending her to a boarding-school where she will have other children around her all the time . . . ?'

But Maxine had gone too far; Mark got up

and strode over to the alcove of plants in the corner of the room. His brooding, angry face told Maxine of her mistake; his voice was angry too. 'Maxine, you have mentioned boarding-school for Emma once before. You know my feelings about it. I will never ever send her away; you know that. Please don't mention it again. If Helen does leave, and I don't think for a moment that she will, then when the time comes then I will consider it, and I will decide the best thing to do. At the moment Emma is happy and settled and I don't want things changed, so if you don't mind we will change the subject and not bring it up again. In fact I will change the subject by telling you that it is Helen's birthday next week and I wondered if we could think of some way of celebrating.'

Maxine was wise enough to hide her feelings and to disguise her chagrin at having Helen brought more prominently into the conversation. She thought for a moment. 'How about you and I, and Neil and Helen making up a foursome and going out to dinner at that hotel on the way to Leeds? They do a very nice meal and there's dancing afterwards. I would have thought that a girl of Helen's age would enjoy an evening of that kind.' She looked at Mark, wondering what his reaction would be. He was sitting in his chair again, and smiled at her. 'Thank you Maxine, I knew I could rely on you to think of something. I'll mention it to

Helen in the morning. Although,' he continued doubtfully, 'she may prefer an evening on her own with Neil.'

The two in question were on their way over to Wedderdale. As the car wound down into the little village of Killingholme and the first lights of the evening could be seen, Helen was reminded of the last time she had experienced the magic of the moor at night and had looked with Mark at the lights of Hexton and Garthdale. She sat quietly at Neil's side as he negotiated the bends and couldn't but help compare the two men. In Neil's company there was always an unruffled enjoyment; he was kindly attentive to her, never changing his mood, ever calm and considerate; she felt a sense of dependability and steadfastness. She knew that a lot of these qualities were missing in Mark as a person, although she realised that as a doctor he displayed the very characteristics she had come to admire in Neil. But did she know Mark as a person? She had seen so many sides of him, and knew deep down in her subconscious that every facet of his personality had the power to stir her in a way that nice, comfortable Neil did not. Inwardly reproaching herself she wondered if she would ever be satisfied, running away from Mark at the first hint of passion, and yet missing something in Neil because he treated her so differently.

She had been lost in thought for so long that

she had not noticed that they had reached Killingholme and that Neil was parking outside the old inn where they often came in an evening for a meal in the comfortable timbered bar. As the car stopped, Neil turned to her and grinned. 'It's not quite dark, shall we go for a walk first and eat afterwards or the other way round?'

Helen chose to walk first and they set off down the village street in the direction of the towered church which stood at one end. A footpath ran alongside the church, across a meadow to the river. Helen had come to learn and take delight in the fact that wherever you went in the Dales you were never far from a river or stream, and Neil had introduced her to some lovely walks always within the sound of water running lightly over the stones. Neil seemed quieter than usual that evening and as they crossed the meadow he took her hand and held it close. The gesture was unlike him. To Helen he had seemed and behaved like a brother and his lack of seeking closer physical contact had endeared him to her rather than the opposite.

He helped her over the narrow footbridge that spanned the river and once on the other side guided her to the large stones under the trees, where they sat watching the water in the growing dusk. Helen felt tranquil and content and thought that Neil must feel the same, so that when his words came they were all the more of a shock to her.

He had kept his arm round her shoulder, and she felt his head bend towards her until his lips touched her soft hair.

'Helen.' His voice was muffled. 'Helen, I've been wanting to say this for a long time. All these weeks you have made me so happy, I wish it could go on for ever. Helen, will you marry me? I love you so much.'

His fingers were under her chin and he tipped her face towards him to meet her lips in a gentle, long kiss. She broke away in confusion and buried her face against the rough wool of his jersey. She had to find words, but could not; she knew in her heart she was very fond of Neil but never had she dreamt of anything more. Startled and bewildered at the love she had engendered in him, she did not know how to tell him that she did not feel the same. He was still holding her close and whispered her name—the word was a query and was needing an answer. She looked up at him.

'Neil,' she said, 'Neil, I'm sorry, I don't know what to say. I enjoy being with you so much, but I've not thought of marriage. It seems only a few weeks since we first met . . .'

Neil stopped her. 'Don't say any more. I've spoken too soon. I should have waited, but I couldn't. You don't dislike me, I know you don't. If we go on seeing one another, perhaps in time you will come to love me too. But I promise I won't keep asking you. Please say you feel we can go on just as we did before.' His voice was full of pleading and Helen didn't have the heart to tell him that she didn't think she would ever feel for him in the way he wanted. But her emotions were so confused that at the same time that she was rejecting him, a voice that seemed to be one of caution was making her wonder if in time she might come to love him enough to marry him. She answered him with some misgiving. 'I would miss you too much to say I won't see you, so I am being very selfish. I don't know how I feel, so if you can put up with me not saying yes, and not saying no, perhaps we can go on just being friends.'

Her words seemed to satisfy him, and he gave her a quick hug, that somehow held relief and hope; he had not lost her altogether.

Helen laughingly changed the subject by saying she was hungry and they went back to the inn for a pleasant meal and a companionable evening.

Next day as she prepared for surgery, she was still thinking of Neil and the morning seemed to have brought misgivings that there would ever be the same easy relationship between them again.

'Helen.' She looked up when she heard her name spoken to meet Mark's intent gaze. He had come into the waiting-room without her even being aware of his presence. As though he had been reading her thoughts he went on to speak about Neil. 'I know it's your birthday next week, and Maxine and I wondered if you would like to celebrate by making a foursome for a dinner and dance—with Neil of course.'

Surprise must have sounded in Helen's voice as she replied; it was not like Maxine to give any thought to her or Neil. 'Well, yes, thank you. It would be very nice. I'll ask Neil. Thank you very much.' She knew she was stammering and he gave her a quick nod and turned away to go to his room saying that they would make the arrangements nearer the time.

Helen grinned ruefully to herself; life suddenly seemed to have become very complicated. She wondered how Mark had known about her birthday; she supposed the date of birth must have been on the medical card that she had given him. But the idea of the foursome was quite pleasing to her and would solve the problem of spending the evening alone with Neil on her birthday.

By the end of the week, arrangements had been made for the night out. Her birthday, which was on 10th May, dawned sunny and bright. She got down to the kitchen for breakfast to find Emma impatient with excitement; there were two parcels on her plate. Mrs Rose smiled birthday wishes and hoped she would have a happy day. 'I think you had better open Miss Emma's parcel first before she tells you what it is.'

The opening of the small gift gave her much pleasure and the sharing of her birthday in such a pleasant manner made her feel younger rather than older. As the pretty paper came away from the small box, Emma whispered, 'We got it at the Gallery.' Knowing that Maxine had only the finest of designs, both of prints and ornaments, Helen was not surprised to find inside the box a small unglazed pottery hedgehog. The appealing creature reflected Emma's love of the countryside and Helen went round the table to give the small girl a hug and a kiss. 'It's lovely, Emma. Thank you very much. You can help me find a special place for it in a minute. But first I must open my other parcel.'

She had just discovered a box of soaps from Mrs Rose and had given that pleased lady a thank you kiss, when she felt hands on her shoulders from behind, as a light kiss dropped on top of her head. 'I don't see why Mrs Rose should have all the kisses,' laughed Mark. 'Happy birthday, Helen.' He sounded cheerful and boyish, and as he put a small parcel in front of her she again had that feeling of discovering yet another part of the man who made up Mark Sinclair. She smiled across at him as he took his seat at the breakfast table, and started to open the package, which was obviously a piece of jewellery. She lifted the top and gave a gasp of delight. Inside was a small pendant on a silver chain; it was a beautifully designed and enamelled flower on a soft brown background.

'It's beautiful,' she breathed, smiling with pleasure. 'I don't know how to thank you.'

Mark was looking at her radiant face. She was so young; his heart stirred and sighed within him with a longing for the years he had lost and would never know again. They all admired the pendant and Helen said she would wear it that evening. She looked around the table at the now familiar faces and thought of how in the two months since she had arrived they had all come to know and accept one another.

It was soon time to start morning surgery and she had a busy time ahead as Dr Wharton was on duty. He arrived in the waiting-room, beaming at Helen, and with his hands behind his back. As she spoke to him, he came round the back of the desk, kissed her and gave her a lovely bunch of early roses. The happiness that these people were giving her filled her thoughts for the whole day, and in no time she was preparing herself for the evening out and putting on a soft wool dress of pale green. The pendant looked perfect against it, but little did she realise the extent of her charm as she joined Mark and Neil who were waiting in the hall. Maxine was the last to arrive, elegant and sophisticated in a black and white suit, and the four of them were soon speeding out of the dale.

At the hotel Mark had booked a table in the window, and as they sat down the last of the day's sunshine caught the tops of the trees in the lovely garden and turned into pure gold the late daffodils growing on the lawn.

It was a pleasant meal, the food was excellent, and Maxine went out of her way to charm Neil, while keeping a proprietorial air in all that she said to Mark. The two men were in jovial mood, and Helen would not have believed that either of them, usually so serious, had such a cheerful and extrovert side to his nature.

Next to the dining-room was a small garden-room laid with a wood-block floor for dancing; it had tables on three sides, one wall being taken up with glass doors opening on to the garden now in darkness. The lights were dimmed and several couples had already taken to the floor. They sat at a table watching the dancers, Mark refusing to dance straight on top of the meal. Helen and Neil laughed at him and were happy to leave the older couple to talk while they started to dance. Helen had always loved dancing and found a good partner in Neil; glancing across the floor at Mark and Maxine she found herself looking straight into Mark's eyes. Maxine was talking but Mark's thoughts were obviously elsewhere. As his gaze met Helen's, he gave a half smile, and she looked away moved by the look more than she cared to admit. She gave her attention to what Neil was saying to her and in a short while Mark and Maxine had joined them on the floor.

As the dance finished and they returned to the table, Maxine once again turned her attention to Neil, keeping him in close conversation about the gallery and the various acquaintances they had in common from the art world. Neil was a keen and talented landscape artist and knew many of the water-colourists who exhibited at the Gallery.

Helen was amused at Maxine's ploy to capture the admiration of both men, and she was quite happy to sit and chat to Mark. When Maxine and Neil got up to dance together, Mark laid his hand over Helen's. Thinking he was going to ask her to dance she started to get up and walk towards the floor, but Mark detained her by a close hold on her hand and suggested that they did not dance but had a walk around the now moonlit garden which lay invitingly outside the long windows. Helen smiled her assent and together they slipped through the glass door and down the steps into the garden. As they walked across the lawn to the cluster of trees and shrubs at the far side of the garden, Mark slipped his arm round Helen's shoulders and they strolled in a friendly silence. Once through the trees they reached a low fence which divided the hotel from the surrounding countryside. Mark stopped and looked over the fence and Helen wondered at his silence. It was almost as though he was trying to weigh up what he was going to say to her. In her imagination she could only think that it would be something to do with Emma and it took her totally by surprise when he started to talk about Neil.

'You see a lot of Neil, don't you, Helen?' She rather resented his tone and the fact that he should question her movements so her answer was defensive. 'Yes, I do go out with him a lot, but I don't see that you have the right to query what I do in my spare time.'

He looked at her stiff face, and wondered, as he had wondered many times, if she were really fond of Neil. He knew that he had no right to lay any claim to where she placed her affections, but somehow it had become important to him to know her feelings. He realised that this was in part a selfish desire not to lose all the good she had done Emma, but he had to admit to himself it was not just that. In the time he had known her he had come to rely on her sensibility and trustworthiness, her tact and cheerfulness were unquestionable, and somehow this little slip of a girl with the long dark hair and fearless, candid eyes, had got under his skin. When he thought of Maxine's predictions he knew he should have been pleased for Helen's sake, that she and the teacher were becoming attached to one another, yet there was present a sense of dismay that somehow he was going to lose her gentle personality before he had even begun to have the chance of knowing her. His next words burst out before he was even aware that he was thinking them.

'You see him nearly every night, you spend every Sunday with him. I've seen Neil looking at you. What does he mean to you?'

Helen looked at him, not believing that it was Mark who had spoken; to her, the words were full of one emotion only, and that was jealousy. But why should he be jealous? They meant nothing to each other and what he had just said filled her with anger that he should suppose he had the right to ask such questions. The anger flared, and had she but known it her usually intent features were filled with a wild and furious beauty that quickened his blood, so that as she replied he hardly heard what she was saying, so aroused were his feelings.

'Mark Sinclair, I think you are impertinent. If you must know I am very fond of Neil and he has asked me to marry him.' She regretted her unguarded reply the moment it was out. Mark stiffened then leaned towards her, grasping both of her arms harshly. She tried to pull away but her struggle infuriated him, and she was pulled roughly into his arms, his lips descending on hers in a deep, savage, demanding kiss from which she could not escape. Her struggles lessened, he pulled her closer still, with one hand stroking her long silky hair, his lips and tongue searching her mouth until her whole body was on fire with response. She willingly gave her lips to his, returning his passion, knowing that she wanted to return it, knowing that she wanted him to go on kissing her for ever.

But ever was not to be then. In a daze they pulled apart, as voices through the trees called their names. Neil appeared followed by Maxine. The latter was no innocent and glanced at the pair before her, noting Mark's quick breathing and Helen's flushed and wild look, her ruffled hair.

'Whatever have you two been up to?' Maxine's voice bristled with anger. 'I don't think it's safe to leave Helen alone with any man. Neil, you'd better take her safely home.'

By this time, Maxine had put her arm through Mark's and did not notice his expression at her malevolent words. She drew Mark slowly to the hotel leaving Helen and Neil to follow. Helen still trembled, but tried to pull herself together and speak to Neil with a semblance of lightness. Her own feelings she shut away, not daring to look them in the face, but feeling still the deep passion of Mark's kiss and feeling, even more, an intense amazement at the desire of her whole body to respond to him.

In the hotel they put their coats on and departed their separate ways. Helen was quiet on the way home, but answered Neil's easy remarks with composure, and he had no suspicion of the tumult going on inside her. She longed to be in the comfort and solitude of her own room, but the evening was not over yet.

As she slipped in the front door of Bridge House, Mark came out to meet her from the kitchen. She wished she had been able to avoid further conversation with him, but tensing herself she went up to him to hear what he wished to say.

'Helen, it's no use my apologising.' Once again the mask of distant politeness had come over him as he stood facing her. 'I understand that you are going to marry Neil, and I hope that you will be very happy. Goodnight.' Turning away, he left her to climb the stairs without giving her the chance to explain the wrong impression she had given him. She sat on her bed, trying to sort out her disordered thoughts; she had made up her mind that she regarded Neil as no more than a good friend, and could not think of him as a future husband, although she had not said as much to him. Now, in her anger she had let Mark think that she was going to marry Neil. He had wished her happiness but in a remote and formal fashion. What did he really feel? Was she reading too much into his ardent kiss and her passionate response? She thought of the two men in her life and how each one affected her in a different way. Comfortable, unpredictable, reliable, infuriating, these were the words that whirled round in her brain and as she dropped off to sleep her last thoughts were of the emotions that Mark had the power to arouse in her, and of a determination to put them to the back of her mind.

## CHAPTER FIVE

Her birthday having ended in a chaos of emotion, Helen spent the rest of that week trying to immerse herself in her work. She had thought that she would be embarrassed to meet Mark every day, but she need not have worried. As before he remained urbane and distant, almost treating her like a stranger. She was glad that she had Emma to think about. The summer term at school had started, Emma having returned eagerly, and Helen enjoyed the afternoon walk up to school to meet her.

On the last day of the week, a particularly fine and warm May day, Emma came across the playground with Jane Elstow by her side and Helen was pleased to see her friend. Knowing that Mrs Rose was planning to take Emma into Leeds to do some shopping the next day, which was a Saturday, Helen suggested that she and Jane had a day out while the weather was fine. Jane was most agreeable and after a little discussion they decided to take the Mini up to Swaledale and have a pub lunch. Helen had not been in that direction before as it was one of the most northerly of the dales.

Saturday dawned fine and clear, and it did not take Helen long to get through the emergency morning surgery. Mark was a little more relaxed in spite of being very tired, and stopped by her desk after the last patient had gone.

'What are you doing with yourself this nice fine weekend?' he enquired. Helen smiled. 'Jane and I are going to Swaledale today, and tomorrow ...' She stopped, half in dismay at what her next words were going to be. But Mark finished for her in an easy manner: ' ... tomorrow you will be seeing Neil. Quite a busy girl.' He studied her for a moment. 'I am glad that you are getting to know the Dales and not missing London too much. Have a nice time.' His tone was almost flippant as he walked off, and Helen shook her head from side to side. Would she ever understand this man? He was not difficult to work for, in fact he made her job very easy, but his character was certainly a mixture of moods and she seemed to see a different side to him every day.

But she wasn't going to let the enigmatic doctor spoil her day's outing. She had a quick coffee, changed into slacks and a casual shirt, slung a jacket over her shoulders and took the

Mini to pick up Jane. It took them about an hour to reach Leyburn where they stopped and found a comfortable pub for lunch. They studied the map after they had finished eating, as it was some time since Jane had been in the area and the roads were completely new to Helen. They took the route over the top of the hill then wound slowly down into Swaledale. They got out of the car on the top to enjoy the glorious view right down the dale and into distant Arkengarthdale.

'You really love it up here, don't you?' remarked Jane.

Helen was slow in replying. 'Yes, it's strange. I was brought up in a lovely county, Dorset, but when you are young I don't think you appreciate the countryside. I couldn't wait to get to London, then after two years there I hated it.'

'It must have been stifling,' agreed Jane. 'I've always lived outside the big towns. I couldn't even bear to work in Leeds like most of my friends did. But I've never known anyone settle into Dales life like you have, you seem to have been here for ever yet it's only been a few months.'

'You know,' said Helen thoughtfully, 'I feel almost as though I belong here. It feels like home to me, and yet I'm a southerner. Perhaps I have been lucky working in the practice and getting to know so many local people.'

Feeling very contented, Helen took the

wheel of the Mini again and they made their way to a small village half way up the dale. Here they had worked out a walk, with the help of the map, that took them right up one side of the dale on a single-track unfenced road. They parked the car, put their walking boots on and set off through the old stone cottages. Soon they were climbing steeply, and taking stops to get their breath back as neither of them was used to a lot of exercise. At the top they sat on the outcrop of rocks that bordered the road and looked around them. Way below them they could see the line of trees that marked the course of the River Swale, and towards the dale head the open expanse of moor that stretched away into the distance above the walled fields.

Helen sighed deeply. 'It really is beautiful; I'm sure there is nowhere in the world like it.'

Jane laughed. 'I don't think the people of Switzerland would agree with you, but it certainly is a lovely spot. I'm surprised that Neil hasn't brought you here.'

There was a note in the other girl's voice that made Helen turn her head, but Jane was serenely taking her fill of the lovely view. Nevertheless the tiny suspicion aroused in Helen's mind was accentuated by Jane's next words. 'He takes you out most Sundays doesn't he?'

'Yes, he is very kind. He has insisted on showing me all round Yorkshire, but we haven't got up here before.' Jane did not seem to want to leave the subject of Neil, and surprised Helen with her next question.

'Do you like him?' Jane was still looking forward into the distance, but the words seemed to hang in the air, fraught with an expectancy and tension. Certain now that her first suspicions were correct and that Jane was thinly disguising her own interest and liking for Neil, Helen replied very carefully. 'Yes, I do like him and he has been very kind to me and to Emma; he is a good companion.' The words left unsaid were meant to imply that there was no more to the friendship than that, in spite of Neil's proposal of marriage. Jane seemed satisfied and turning to Helen she said

'And what about Mark? How do you feel about him?' She wasn't surprised to see the flush rising under Helen's skin as she waited for a reply. When it came it was quick and matter-of-fact. Jane was not to guess what a rush of sudden emotion had surged up in Helen at the mention of Mark's name. She felt annoyance at the strength of her feelings, and her hurried words hid all that she truly felt. 'Oh, Mark. He's fine to work for but he's got Maxine.'

Jane seemed to give an audible sigh of relief. 'I'm glad you feel like that. I wasn't sure about Neil, but I wondered sometimes about you and Mark. The whole town knows that he and Maxine will get married sooner or later

109

and I didn't want you to get hurt.'

Jane's words were light and considerate, but the last sentence made Helen's heart sink, Mark and Maxine. Had she been a blind fool? They were always together, but somehow it had never occurred to Helen that they were thinking about marriage. What about Emma? Maxine had never liked the little girl. And Mark, she could not imagine him, the country loving doctor married to the sophisticated, city-loving Maxine. Why had she never thought of it before, why did it matter so much? Was she thinking about Emma, or did she have to be honest with herself and come face to face with the fact that it was the state of her own heart she was thinking of? She gave herself a little shake. What a muddle, Neil wanting to marry her, Mark thinking she was going to marry Neil, and now Mark and Maxine. Was Jane right? It seemed as though everyone knew about it but her, and she had just ignored all the signals that lay in front of her.

Jane brought her back to the present and the view over Swaledale. 'You seem to be doing a lot of thinking. Hadn't you guessed about Mark and Maxine? You have seen them together often enough.'

'To be honest, I've never thought about it. And I just can't imagine Emma fitting in with the two of them.'

'I think Emma has been the problem all

110

along,' said Jane, 'or I think they would have been married long ago. I've a feeling Maxine wants to send Emma away to boarding-school and I should hate to see that happen. I think she's too young. In any case she's been so much better since you've been here.'

Helen was shocked. 'But surely Mark wouldn't send her away,' she protested. 'It wouldn't be right.'

'I think it's Maxine who would make the decision,' rejoined Jane. 'I shouldn't be talking like this. It's only hearsay, and it's their business after all. But I'm fond of Emma and I would like to see her in a happy home.'

'I couldn't agree more,' Helen replied. 'I want her happiness more than anything.' She was silent once again, then she began to get up. 'You've opened my eyes, Jane, and I'm thankful. I think I've been an idiot not to see which way the wind was blowing. Let's change the subject now and start walking back.' The two girls made their way back down the steep hill into the little village and to the car. Helen drove home quietly and Jane did not make many interruptions. Helen had been given a lot to think about, and when they parted in the square, she was glad to get back to Bridge House. She was pounced upon by Emma as soon as she returned and eagerly shown the purchases from Leeds. She was glad to have tea in the kitchen and if her bedtime hour with Emma was tinged with anxiety, she did not show it.

She thought over what Jane had told her and also thought how unwittingly Jane had revealed that she felt some attachment to Neil. As Helen dwelt upon this, a rather warm comfortable feeling came over her. Although she was fond of Neil, she knew in her heart of hearts that she would never agree to marry him, and the new idea of Jane and Neil was pleasing her. They were both teachers and had similar interests. Helen imagined herself in the role of matchmaker, and the day ended with thoughts of Mark and Maxine pushed to the back of her mind, and plans formulating for getting Jane and Neil together.

Helen was meeting Neil on the following day for their usual Sunday outing and again the weather in the morning showed all the signs of the balmy warmth of early summer. Clear blue skies and the freshest of greens of the trees now coming into leaf heightened the beauty of the countryside that lay beyond the steeper landscape of the dale. They had planned to visit a garden that was open to the public near Ripon. They had visited the cathedral town on another occasion and had planned to return in the summer to see the gardens, which were specially renowned for the beautiful flowering shrubs which graced the parkland.

It being early in the season, there were no great crowds, and Neil and Helen found themselves sitting on a bench amid the first lilacs just coming into bloom. Helen had always thought of the lilac as a mauve or white flower, now for the first time she was able to appreciate the subtle colourings and the hint of the scents to come in the weeks ahead, when the trees would be at their best.

Conversation had been spasmodic between the two, but this never worried Helen as Neil was always relaxed and undemanding. She still had the thought of Jane Elstow at the back of her mind, but had no idea how she would possibly have the opportunity to bring Jane to Neil's notice. It was not, however, in the way that Helen would have expected, or that she would have wished, as Neil dropped his light bantering mood and became serious.

'Helen, I know I said I wouldn't keep asking you, but seeing you and Mark together the other night, made me wonder if there was any chance for me at all. What is there between you and Mark ...?' He was interrupted as Helen, in an agitated way, broke into what he was saying. 'There's nothing between me and Mark, nothing at all. I don't even think Mark likes me very much, although we do work well together. Mark is going to marry Maxine; he's always with her and Jane told me yesterday that it's common knowledge in Hexton that they will soon be married.'

Helen was protesting, but it wasn't helping her in what she knew she would have to say to

Neil if he insisted on an answer. Relief was in his face as he suddenly smiled at her. 'Well if it's not Mark, then do you think you will come to care for me a little? We get on so well, Helen, we never quarrel; please say yes this time.' He was holding her hands and pulling her close and Helen had to summon all her will-power to bring out her next words. 'Neil, I told you before that I do like you. I don't want to hurt you but I just don't feel that way about you. Not to contemplate marriage. I'm sorry, you've been so nice to me, I've really enjoyed going out with you, but I just can't think of you in any other way than as a good friend.'

Helen felt that her words sounded at the same time both feeble and cruel, but it was not in her nature to deceive although she knew that her straightforward honest reply would be deeply hurtful to Neil. He remained silent, trying to overcome his bitter disappointment. He had come to know that Helen was sincere in all she said and did, and he had come to love her, although he knew that he had never stirred in her any emotion that was akin to love. He was still holding her hands, and as he looked at her lovely face, he knew that for the sake of them both it would be better if they stopped seeing one another. Helen must have read his thoughts for her grip tightened and she looked him straight in the eyes and said: 'We won't see each other any more Neil. You must meet other girls, find someone who will love you as you deserve to be loved.' A wild idea came into her head, albeit a foolish one. 'What about Jane Elstow, she's lovely and she's a teacher and you've always had a very high regard for her.'

For a moment she thought she had caught his attention. 'Jane,' he pondered. 'She's a good teacher; I've known her for years ... but she's not you, Helen.'

All Helen would say was 'Still waters run deep'; and Neil, looking at her, quizzically responded 'And what is that supposed to mean?' Helen did not reply and promptly changed the subject, feeling she had already done enough in bringing Jane's name into the conversation at all. Disappointed though he was, Neil was too good-natured to wish Helen ill and got up and pulled her up by the hand and said 'Well, there's one thing certain, I'm not going to quarrel with you. You know where the school is and you come nearly every day; I'm there if you need me and until I see you married to someone else I shall never give up hope.'

As they walked back through the gardens, Helen thought over these last words and thought how perverse she was being. She thought of Mark and how his changes of mood infuriated and perplexed her, and yet given the chance of a life with someone as solid and dependable as Neil, it was not enough for her and she was turning him away.

They said very little on the way home and Neil sadly watched her go up the steps of Bridge House, knowing he had lost her, but at the same time wondering if he had ever known the real Helen. He had a sudden remembrance of her flushed face as she had broken from Mark's embrace on her birthday evening, and in spite of what Helen had said about Maxine, he did not entirely believe the story, and had a strange premonition that Helen and Mark were destined for one another. If that was what Helen wanted, he hoped he was right, it was her happiness that mattered most after all.

Helen's days after her break with Neil were marked by emptiness, yet in all fairness to him she was sure she had done the right thing, and she hoped against hope that something would open his eyes to Jane's true worth and that two would come together. Little did she know that Neil himself, trying not to be heartbroken, was wishing the same for herself and Mark.

Since Jane's disclosures Helen had tried to avoid any close contact or conversation with Mark. She saw him at surgery time; in the evenings when she was in her room, she would hear Maxine's voice downstairs and the slam of the car door as the two drove off. There were not many evenings when Maxine did not appear and each meeting seemed to Helen to reaffirm what Jane had said. As always when she considered the future between Mark and Maxine it was Emma she thought of and it was

Emma who, early the following week, provoked a chain of happenings which Helen could not have foreseen.

She was in the kitchen having lunch with Mrs Rose when their conversation was interrupted by the ringing of the telephone. Helen usually answered it, but Mrs Rose told her to finish her lunch and hurried off to the waiting-room herself. Seconds later she was shouting 'Helen, come quickly. It's Mr Brandon. It's Miss Emma.'

Wondering at Mrs Rose's almost hysterical voice, Helen rushed to the phone, it was not like Mrs Rose to be upset if Emma had run away. She picked up the phone and heard Neil's calm voice. 'Helen, I'm afraid there's been an accident. Emma was skipping in the playground after lunch, and I gather from the girls who were turning the rope, that her feet got caught and she fell and hit her head badly. I think you'd better come straight away. She's unconscious. We've rung for the ambulance.'

Panic rose in Helen's breast but she tried not to show it. 'Will she have to go to hospital?'

'Yes, I should certainly think so. You'd better bring a bag of night-clothes and things if you can pick them up quickly.' Neil put the phone down and the click triggered Helen into action. Hastily she told Mrs Rose what had happened, she tore upstairs to Emma's room fetching a small holdall from her own, on the

117

way. She grabbed everything she could think of, glanced over Emma's bed, saw Moocher, picked him up and stuffed him on top of the bag. She knew he had become Emma's comfort toy.

She ran all the way to the school to find Neil waiting for her at the entrance. He put his arm round her. 'You must be prepared for a shock; she's not looking too good.' He took her into his room where she found Jane bending over a small still figure under a blanket on a camp-bed. In spite of Neil's warning she drew in her breath sharply when she saw Emma's face. It was motionless and deathly white, the graze on her head standing out vividly against her pale skin. But it was the stillness that gave Helen the greatest shock. Jane held out her hand as Helen stammered: 'But she looks, she looks . . . is she still alive?'

'Feel her pulse,' Jane directed her. 'It is quite strong, she's knocked herself out completely.'

As Helen bent over the child, the ambulance men arrived and it took some of the numbness away to let them take charge. They moved her carefully and she was soon in the ambulance with Helen climbing in to join her. Neil and Jane stood side by side and she called to them, 'Try and get in touch with Mark; he's out on his round somewhere; Mrs Rose will be able to find him.' She turned to the hospital men. 'Which hospital are we going to?'

'Leeds General,' was the reply. 'It's the nearest.' Neil promised to find Mark, the doors were shut and they were off. It was the longest ride that Helen ever remembered in her life; Leeds was not that far away but once they reached the edge of the built-up area, progress seemed to become slower in spite of the ambulance's warning siren. Helen sat staring at the white face and holding Emma's hand; the ambulance man had his finger on the child's pulse. The arrival at the big hospital, the examination by the doctor, the X-ray, and then moving Emma to a small room at the end of a ward, all passed in a daze to Helen. When Emma was finally settled in the bed and a nurse was posted to sit with her, Helen sat on the other side still stunned, a sense of unreality, a feeling that it was not her sitting there and above all not being able to think how the small, unmoving child could possibly be the vibrant eight-year old she knew so well. She thought of Mark and in her imagination was following him around his afternoon calls. She could remember most of them and knew that Mrs Rose would find the rota and try every patient until she was able to contact him. One call was to an old lady with bronchitis at the head of the dale, and Helen realised that if he had got as far as that it would be a long time before he reached the hospital. The afternoon dragged on, but there was no change in Emma. Helen was getting more and more anxious, and longing for Mark's calm presence, when the door quietly opened and he slipped into the room. He stood at the foot of the bed gazing at his daughter with an unfathomable look. Moving closer he checked her pulse and laid his hand on her cheek. He sat by Helen, touched her arm and in a quiet voice asked her to tell him what had happened.

'I was up at Mrs Buckle's when I got the message, but Mrs Rose couldn't tell me much, only to come straight here.'

'I guessed that was where you would be,' answered Helen. 'When you didn't come, I remembered you had to see old Mrs Buckle. But I knew you would come as quickly as you could.' She told him as much as she knew and he listened, quietly nodding. 'It may be only simple concussion, a playground is a very hard surface for a knock on the head and she must have gone down with quite a crash. But the doctor tells me that fortunately there is no sign of a fracture of the skull.'

Their conversation was interrupted by the nurse bringing them tea which they both drank thankfully.

'What about afternoon surgery?' asked Helen. 'It's nearly half-past four now.'

'It's all right, I managed to get hold of Dr Wharton. He was at home and he did the one remaining call at Smurthwaite and then went back to Bridge House. He was very upset, he has always been especially fond of Emma, ever since,' he hesitated, 'ever since her mother left us. We needn't worry about surgery at all, we'll stay here and hope that Emma regains consciousness soon.'

Helen derived solid comfort from the use of the word 'we' and the real fright that had been with her all the afternoon lessened now that she had Mark by her side.

They had eaten sandwiches and coffee, and sat tense and waiting, saying very little to each other, when the first sign of movement came from Emma. It was hardly a movement, just a slow opening of her eyes, but she seemed to see nothing. Mark went closer; she started to say something, her voice weak but clear, and her first word sent a chill right through Helen.

'Mummy. I want my Mummy.'

There was pain in Mark's voice as he whispered his reply. 'It's Daddy, Emma.'

'No, no. Mummy. I want Mummy,' the voice began to rise, and to Helen's horror, Mark buried his head in his hands. She knew she must help and move beside him, trying again to speak to Emma with urgency and command in her young voice. 'Emma. It's Helen. Can you see me Emma?' There was only silence from the bed and suddenly Helen started talking, clearly, quickly, anything that came into her head. Anything that would break through the consciousness of the small child.

'Emma. It's Helen. You know Helen. I always put you to bed and we read a story. Emma, I've got Moocher. He was sitting on your bed so I brought him to see you. Can you hear me Emma? It's Helen. I love you Emma, please try to speak to me.'

Helen had never taken her eyes from Emma's face and with a horror she would never forget she saw the eyelids close. She turned to Mark, flung herself into his arms and buried her face on his shoulder. In desperation he held her tight, then with one hand lifted her head so that he could see her tear-filled eyes. 'Listen. Helen, listen.'

The nurse had come to their side of the bed. 'Dr Sinclair, her pulse is stronger, she has gone into a natural sleep, I will call the doctor.'

When he came the hospital doctor was equally reassuring. 'She will be all right now. She will probably sleep for a long time but the crisis is over. I will leave Nurse to make arrangements for you to stay the night if you wish to.'

Helen was still sitting within the circle of Mark's arms; she felt an overwhelming sense of relief at the doctor's words, but found that her whole body was reacting to the strain of the last few hours and was so exhausted and drained that she could not move. But for Mark's arms she felt she would have fallen across the bed. Both Mark and the nurse were looking at her, and the nurse was the first to

122

speak. 'If you are going to wait up all night with her I think it would be best if one of you had a lie down. I shall be going off duty at eight but there will be another nurse here for the night.' Then she heard Mark's voice close to her ear. 'You are going to have a rest now and try and sleep for a few hours. I am used to being up in the night and will be able to stay awake quite easily.' Slowly he led her to a long cushioned couch, obviously kept in the room for relatives, and Helen did not protest. Thankfully she lay down, and did not know how long she had slept when she heard Mark's urgent calling. 'Helen, wake up. Emma is asking for you. It seems that I won't do.'

She sat up wide awake, and in a second was back by the bed, to hear the plaintive cry. 'Helen. Helen.'

She held the girl's hand and bent towards her. 'Yes, Emma, it's Helen here.'

'Helen, I want a drink.' The night nurse moved forward and gave Emma a sip from a feeding mug, but the little voice went on. 'Helen, where's Moocher? Can I have him?' Helen turned and Mark silently handed the old woollen dog to her and she put him where Emma could touch him with her hand. The next words sounded a bit more sleepy but were still sensible. 'Helen, can I have a real dog one day?' There could be only one reply and Helen made it. 'Yes, you can, Emma. Go to sleep now.' The eyelids dropped again and Emma drifted into the health-giving sleep of recovery.

In relief Helen turned back to Mark; it was a tortured gaze that met hers. Her arms went out to him and he seemed glad to cling to her. 'It was you she wanted; what use am I to her? It was you she wanted,' he repeated.

Helen was gentle and laid her cheek against his. 'Mark, I think it was because my voice was the last one she heard before she went into that deep sleep. She remembered Moocher, didn't she?' As she continued she tried to be practical to assuage his distress. 'Mark, you're tired and you've got morning surgery. Why don't you go home now and have a few hours sleep? You've got a busy day in front of you. I've had a rest, you haven't and I can sit with Emma. She is in a nice sleep now. She will be all right . . . oh, but how will you manage if I'm not there?'

He almost gave the ghost of a laugh and hugged her. 'I think I'm capable of getting out the notes and fetching the patients myself. The typing can wait. You are right, there's no need for two of us here and I think it's you she will need when she wakes up.' He sounded so forlorn that Helen put a hand up to caress the side of his face, and he nestled into her palm as though it gave him comfort. Then bending over Emma, he dropped a kiss on her white brow and went silently from the small room.

Helen sat immobile. Her relief at Emma's regaining consciousness was mingled with an agony of pity for Mark. She tried to think it out, and came to the realisation that over the last few months she had been the companion in Emma's happiness. She was the one to fetch her from school, to put her to bed and to take her for walks. Mark was never consciously unkind to Emma, but he seemed unable to show affection, whether out of grief for his lost wife or from some inner restraint. Whatever the reason for Mark's lack of closeness to his daughter, the effect had been the same. Emma had turned to Helen when the mother she called for, and obviously still yearned for, was not there.

Bringing her back to the present surroundings, the nurse touched her arm—she had brought coffee and some toast. 'Oh, I couldn't eat now,' was Helen's reaction.

The young nurse was firm and understanding. 'I know you don't feel like it, but it may be hours before Emma wakes again and you need to have something inside you.' Helen sipped the hot, strong coffee, felt revived and while the nurse talked to her quietly, found that she had eaten the toast and she felt better. 'Thank you,' she said. 'You were right, I did need it.' Looking at the child lying in the bed, a worried look came into her face. 'She is going to recover isn't she?'

The nurse was hesitant. 'Well it's not for me to give an opinion, you should really talk to the doctor next time he comes round. But the fact that she has woken up and had a drink and gone to sleep again is a good sign. I will leave you now, just ring the bell if you are worried or if Emma wakes up.'

The night dragged on into morning, and Helen had a little sleep in her chair. Her talk with the doctor was reassuring, and she managed to eat a light lunch and settle down and watch the pale child again. The nurse had brought her a pile of magazines, but she lacked the power of concentration. She could only sit and think, her thoughts a maelstrom, racing through her mind and giving her no peace— Emma, Mark, Neil, Maxine, Jane. Nothing seemed clear.

Soon after lunch the door opened and Mark crept in, put his fingers to his lips and went straight up to Emma. He put his fingers on the young girl's pulse, his training automatically noting her even breathing and her slightly improved colour. He sat down by Helen's side still holding Emma's hand. In a whisper he said, 'Has she woken again?'

Helen shook her head. 'No, but in the last half hour she has moved once or twice and I don't think she is in quite such a deep sleep.'

Mark considered. 'It's nearly eight hours since she woke. Speak to her Helen, she may hear you.' Helen called Emma's name softly and firmly. There was no response.

'Try again.'

'Emma, it's Helen. Daddy has come to see

you.'

Helen waited anxiously. If only, she thought, Emma would open her eyes while Mark was here; the strain and tension in his face worried her. She kept calling Emma's name but still there was no response. She took Mark's hand and held it hard; she didn't know what to do. She had no idea how serious Emma's head injury was, and she knew that Mark would recognise signs that she knew nothing about; when she looked at the still little figure her heart plummeted. She looked at Mark, willing him to tell her why Emma could not hear them, and that it had no desperate significance. 'Why doesn't...'

'Sh, sh.' Mark unclasped her hand and quickly took Emma's wrist. 'I think she is waking.'

Helen looked at the bed and saw Emma making slight movements of the head; then her hand went up to touch her forehead; the fingers felt the dressing and at the same time she opened her eyes. She looked around as though not seeing anything and Helen held her breath. The eyes rested on Mark's face. 'Daddy,' the thin, weak voice said. 'Where am I? What are you doing here?'

The tears rolled down Helen's face and she got up and walked to the foot of the bed leaving Mark to bend over Emma, holding her hands and talking to her gently. He must have mentioned Helen's name for Emma looked

127

around again and recognised the figure standing near.

'Helen, Daddy says I fell down in the playground when I was skipping but I don't remember anything about it. I'm not at home, this is the hospital, isn't it . . . ?'

Mark had to stop her talking, he gave her a drink and the nurse and the doctor came in. As Helen watched the consultation, the sense of relief was so great that she felt weak and sat down once again by the bed. She couldn't understand a lot of what was said between the two doctors, but one look at Mark's face gave her hope. The tiredness was still there in his expression, but the intense anxiety had gone and she recognised the patient, understanding look that he had in the surgery.

Emma was asleep once more, and when the nurse and doctor had gone Mark sat down with Helen. His voice was calm as he looked at her. 'We think it is straightforward concussion and that there is no injury to the brain. She will have to have a scan before we know for certain, but I think we can be hopeful. Helen, I'm going to ask you to stay at the hospital. They will give you a bed at night.' When she started to protest he interrupted her. 'You are not to worry about the practice. Sheila's baby isn't due for another four weeks and I will ask her to come back for a few mornings. Emma needs you. You will do it for me, won't you—and for Emma?'

Helen could not refuse and as she murmured her assent, he took her shoulders in both hands and kissed the top of her head. 'Bless you, I don't know what I'd do without you.' With these words he was gone, leaving Helen a lot happier but still with a knot of worry about Emma's condition. When the nurse came in, Helen asked if she could possibly have a wash, and she was shown a tiny room with just a bed and chair and wash-basin in it. She was told it would be hers until Emma was well enough to be left. The nurse had no idea how long this would be; she was used to nursing children and Helen found it encouraging to have someone to talk to and to share her worries.

## CHAPTER SIX

Emma stayed in the hospital for a week. For the first two nights Helen slept in the little room next to the small ward and sat with Emma during the day. As Emma recovered she was at first fretful and demanding and Helen found the days very tiring. Mark came every evening and Helen, thinking it best to leave the two of them together, took the opportunity to have a short walk in the hospital grounds. It was the only time she was able to get out for any fresh air and exercise.

Mark kept his visits short but each time he came he appeared to be very pleased with Emma's progress. The scan had shown up no internal injury much to everyone's relief, and soon Emma was getting lively and there was no need for Helen to stay the night. On the third day Mark took Helen back with him so that she could return with the Mini on the following morning. Emma had been moved into the general children's ward and was happy and content with all the company and attention she was getting.

As Helen got into the Range Rover on the evening that he took her back to Hexton, she thought how close they had become during the crisis of Emma's illness. There seemed to be an easiness between them that hadn't been there before, and it was a pleasure to Helen to see the lines on Mark's face gradually relax. He was laughing as he started the car.

'She didn't mind us going one bit, did she? I think she's going to get thoroughly spoilt. We shall have our hands full when she comes home.' Helen agreed. 'She has got better very quickly. It doesn't seem possible that it's only three days since we were sick with worry, does it?'

Mark was concentrating on a roundabout that led them out on to the main road from Leeds to Hexton, but as soon as they were on the fast dual-carriageway, he glanced down at the girl sitting by his side. She seemed to fit in, and yet he remembered the intimation that her intentions lay in Neil's direction; the knowledge gave him a pang of regret. She had done so much for Emma—his thoughts were leaping away from him in a future that might include Helen. Yet again he remembered Neil and stifled the half-formulated stirrings of feeling that had swept over him. His musings did not stop him from voicing his praise of this practical, lovely girl who had become so fond of his daughter. 'I shall never be able to thank you for what you have done for Emma. Her recovery is mainly due to your love for her and your patience.'

Helen was able to reply sincerely: 'You don't have to thank me, Mark, it is enough for me to know that she is better. I shall look forward to having her home in a few days time and getting back to the old routine. I have missed the surgery.' Mark noticed her use of the word home, so naturally she had said it, and again he felt that pang of regret but made no comment. They were soon turning off the main road to the narrow country lane that led to Hexton, there was a lot of traffic about and Mark needed to pay attention at some of the dangerous bends, so very little was said for the rest of the journey.

The next few days seemed to Helen to be one long rush. She saw to the morning surgery, then drove to the hospital leaving Sheila to cope in the afternoons. She came home again at tea-time and Mark visited in the evenings, but as far as Helen could see Maxine didn't go. She heard her voice rather petulantly trying to detain Mark one evening but he had no time for her and rushed off to see Emma. He could have taken Maxine with him but in Helen's imagination, visiting a sick child in hospital was not really the older woman's scene and Mark's insistence on going every evening was not to her liking.

The day that Emma came home there was relief and rejoicing from all sides. Helen brought her at tea-time, but nothing could persuade the lively child to go to bed, even though the doctor at the hospital had said she should be kept as quiet as possible for a few more days. In the end she agreed to be tucked up quietly in the big arm-chair in Helen's room until it was bed-time. It was there that she was found by Maxine on the first evening home. Fully expecting to regain Mark's attentions now that Emma was better, she had prepared to be charming and magnanimous to the small girl who occupied no place in her affections.

Helen was sitting on a small stool by Emma's chair when Mark and Maxine appeared in the doorway. There was no welcoming smile on Emma's face as Maxine went up to her and said in her strident voice: 'Well, Emma, that was a silly thing to do wasn't it?'

The words dropped into a startled silence.

Helen watched Mark's face and caught first a look of bewilderment and then disbelief. He remained silent struggling for words. He started as though to say something but only gave the impression that he was trying to bite back his words. He went over to Emma, who by the end of the day got very tired, and noted the scowl on her face. 'Cheer up, Emma,' he said, trying to speak lightly. 'Maxine has brought you a present.'

'I don't want it.' The sound of the cross voice brought an embarrassed silence to the room. Maxine was affronted, and Mark annoyed at Emma's rudeness, so Helen thought it time to step in.

'I'll undo the paper for you Emma. I've a feeling it's one of your favourite things.' The parcel revealed a lovely jig-saw, a round one, featuring the small creatures and wild flowers of the English countryside. Helen handed it over to Emma, who took it without showing any interest but managed a grudging, 'Thank you.' Maxine turned toward the door.

'Come along, Mark.' She seemed at her most distant and forbidding. 'I think we had better leave Emma to Helen's tender care.' The unpleasant sneer to her words caused Helen to look at Mark, and as their eyes met there seemed to be a deep sympathy between them; on Helen's part a pleading look that begged to excuse Emma's bad behaviour, and on his side an unspoken appeal in his eyes

133

which Helen was at a loss to interpret.

The next day's visit was of a different order altogether. Emma had been allowed up during the day and had been happy sitting at the kitchen table with Mrs Rose doing her jig-saw, while Helen was busy in the waiting-room. There was a lot of work to catch up on and she was pleased to leave Emma in Mrs Rose's care until after tea, when once again they went up to Helen's room. Mark had popped in for a friendly chat and to say goodnight; if he remembered the embarrassing scene of the night before, he showed no sign of disapproval of his daughter, though it was noticeable that Maxine did not put in an appearance before they went off together.

It was almost Emma's bedtime when there came a hesitant knock on the door, and when Helen opened it she was filled with delight to find Neil and Jane standing there. Emma's excitement and self-importance knew no bounds at having not only her own teacher, but the head-master to visit her, and the four of them spent a happy, laughing half-hour playing one of Emma's games. As Helen said goodbye to them she was thoughtful; had Emma's accident brought the two together? She would like to think so, but told herself to be patient and to await events.

In a few days time, Emma was pronounced fit and well and able to go out. The only sign of her mishap was the healing graze on her forehead. At the weekend, Helen was able to take her for a walk along the river, it now being the first week in June and quite warm. On the Monday Emma was back at school and the comfortable routine between practice and school once more established itself.

A few weeks after this, Helen took the first time off since she had been in Hexton, and travelled down to Dorset to visit her parents. Sheila had had her baby, so she could not run the waiting-room, but as only a Friday and Saturday were involved Mark and Mrs Rose assured her that they could manage between them.

Mark drove her into the station at Leeds and saw her off. As they drove along he started to talk about holidays, asking Helen if she had any plans.

'Maxine and I have talked about having a week in the Channel Islands in the school holidays, but we've done nothing about it. I wasn't sure how you would manage.' Mark sounded contrite. 'I'm sorry, Helen, I should have mentioned it before. What I am going to try and do is get a young married locum, whose wife will run the waiting room for me. I've done that other years and it's worked very well.'

Helen looked at him enquiringly 'What about Emma? Do you take her anywhere on holiday?'

Mark nodded 'Maxine and I usually have a

couple of weeks somewhere, while the locum is here, and we take Emma with us.' He sounded rather dubious. 'I can't say that Emma really enjoys it, though we always go to the sea for her sake. But for some reason she doesn't really like Maxine very much and we generally have a few troublesome moments. However it's the best I can do. I'm afraid it means that you will be tied to having the same weeks as I do, so I hope that you will be able to fix something up.'

Helen thanked him, and had the secret thought that she wished she could take Emma somewhere, but she knew it would be considered interference and decided to say nothing.

Helen enjoyed the weekend with her parents, spending some time with her sister and her two small children, and together they visited some of their favourite Dorset beauty spots.

She returned to Bridge House late on the Sunday evening, and opened the front door to hear raised voices coming from upstairs. She thought that Emma's shrill piping was amongst them, and was surprised as Emma should have been in bed hours ago.

She stood in the hall, bag in hand, when there was a loud shout.

'I've had enough of you. You can't wait up for Helen. Will you do what I say and go to bed! Goodnight!' Howls and cries from

Emma's bedroom were followed by a furious Maxine stamping down the stairs. When she saw Helen she stopped. 'There you are!' she shouted. 'About time too! I can't do a thing with that brat! Mark's been called out, Mrs Rose hasn't returned from her sister's, and all Emma will say is that she won't go to bed until she has seen Helen. Will you take over? I'm going to get myself a drink and I hope I don't see either of you again this evening.' At these last words the front door opened and Mark came in. He had obviously heard some of what Maxine had said, but chose to ignore her and went to Helen and took her bag.

'I'm glad to see you back, Helen. I'll carry your bag upstairs, and perhaps you wouldn't mind settling Emma. I'm afraid she hasn't been very good while you've been away.'

Maxine was bursting with fury because Mark had spoken to Helen first.

'The child's spoilt.' Her tone was a little quieter as though she realised how her outburst must have sounded to Mark. She turned to him as he came back down the stairs, and said, 'Helen will cope with her now, Mark, let's have a drink.' They went into the lounge together.

Upstairs in Emma's room, a ball of energy threw itself at Helen nearly knocking her over.

'Oh, Helen. You've come back. Please don't ever go away again and leave me with Maxine. I hate her. I hate her.' Helen held the child

137

close, she wanted to hug and hug her, but knew that she mustn't let the last words go unheeded.

'Emma, your Daddy tells me you've been naughty. And you must never talk like that about anyone.' The child had buried her head in Helen's dress. She found it difficult to find the right words; words which a small girl of Emma's age would understand. She said gently as she held Emma tightly. 'Loving things is good. You love Mrs Rose, don't you?' Emma nodded. 'But hating is bad. We must never hate people. There are all sorts of things we don't like but we have to learn not to mind too much, and then they don't seem so bad.' She was making a hopeless mess of it but she could see the intelligent little girl was thinking hard, and her next words, while they almost made Helen laugh, at the same time, made her realise that Emma was really trying to understand.

'It's like Benjy Ruffles,' she announced, and then explained herself. 'He always used to take our ball in the playground, and we got cross and hated ... er didn't like him. Then Miss Elstow told us not to take any notice, and we didn't, and he wasn't so bad after that.'

Helen heaved a sigh of relief at the change of subject and Emma's perception. She soon had Emma in bed and told her about the niece and nephew she had seen while she was away; the weary, overwrought girl soon relaxed and

138

was fast asleep, leaving Helen to ponder over what had happened.

It was early in the evening of the next day that the aftermath of these events made itself known. Mark had been quiet all day as though he had something on his mind, and somehow it was no surprise to hear, when she came downstairs from settling Emma, that he wanted to talk to her.

She went into his room and felt rather nervous as she sat facing him across his desk, though what caused the feeling of apprehension she could not say. Perhaps it was his stern, worried look, his creased brow.

'Helen, it's no use hiding the fact that I've got something on my mind. You are involved and I feel it's only fair to ask your opinion.'

She looked at him mystified, but remained silent. He continued; 'I hardly need to tell you that it's Emma. You saw how she behaved with Maxine last night and she has been like it all the time you have been away.' For a moment he looked apologetic. 'I know that Maxine is not used to small children, she's never had any of her own. But she is a good woman, a very successful and charming businesswoman. It seems to me that the environment that Emma lives in, always surrounded by adults, is not doing her any good, though I will admit since you have been here, she has been much better.'

This last sentence should really have given

Helen a clue to what was coming, but it didn't and when Mark's next words were spoken it was like a bombshell exploding inside her.

'We, Maxine and I, have talked it over and we think that it would be in Emma's best interests if she was sent away to school.'

To say that Helen was speechless would be an understatement. She could not believe that Mark had said it; he was looking at her waiting for a reply.

She stood up and faced him across the desk. 'School, boarding-school, I suppose you mean,' she screamed at him. 'How can you even think of such a thing, it's not hard to guess whose idea it was.' He put up his hand to stop her, but her fury, her anguish for Emma's sake was so great that nothing would stop her and she didn't care what she said. 'Oh, you doctors,' she continued remorselessly, 'You think you're so clever, but you're so clinical! Haven't you any emotion, any understanding? Don't you know the word love? A child needs love, not sending away to school! It's the most crazy idea I ever heard! Emma has a good home, someone to give her tea, someone to meet her from school, someone to put her to bed. She is not a deprived child in that sense, but she is deprived nevertheless. Her mother has gone, but in Emma's little heart how can she know or not whether she will ever see her mother again? She still grieves, yet have you ever seen her cry in front of you? Have you never heard it said that a child who is emotionally deprived cannot cry? Her eyes tell it all, yet how often do you look down into them to read their message? If you did, you would see how much she needs that love and affection, that care, that tenderness! The love that should come from a mother or a father. But no, you are too busy, you leave it to others ...' she stopped abruptly. Mark was sitting transfixed, staring at her. Appalled, horrified at her outburst, she dashed the tears from her eyes, turned and fled from the room. In the hall she grabbed her raincoat, in seconds she was down the steps of Bridge House, and running all the way to the bridge and across into the meadow. Hardly stopping at the river, she ignored the riverside footpath and took the steep track that led up to the moor.

The lower part of the track led through a thick clump of trees, and coming out of the bright light into the cover of their thick foliage seemed to have the effect of cooling her anger. She slowed her furious pace, which in any case was having disastrous effects on her breathing, and finding a broad oak leaned against its solid trunk and shut her eyes. But she could not think properly, her emotion, her anger, her love for Emma, were so hideously entangled that it had the effect of making her mind totally blank. She tried to think and the only thing that came to her mind was the pile of rocks where she often stopped when she took the car up the road that divided Garthdale from Wedderdale. It was always a soothing, peaceful place to be, and it was just what she needed.

'I could climb up there,' she said to herself. 'It's only just gone seven and at this time in June it doesn't get dark till eleven o'clock.' The thought of the walk and the soothing sanctuary at the top calmed her and when she set off again it was with a steady pace that soon took her out of the trees and into the first of several meadows she had to cross before she reached the open moor. She followed the footpath making carefully for each snicket in the walls that marked the way from one field to another. The gaps in the wall followed each other in an almost direct line making progress easy as she climbed higher. Her weekend walking with Neil and then with Jane had served well to make her an experienced walker on the upper slopes, though she regretted that she had only thin walking shoes on and not her proper walking boots. However, the ground was dry after the warm sunny spell, and although it was not a sunny evening the cloud cover was only light and it didn't look as though it was going to rain. She almost wished she had not brought her raincoat; she did not need it for warmth and it was a nuisance to have to carry it.

When she came through the last of the snickets she looked up at the moor, knowing which direction she wanted to go but unable to see the stones. The top of the moor seemed a long way away, but anger had heightened her determination and she set off firmly on the broad bridle path. It was easy walking and she started to enjoy herself. As she climbed higher she kept stopping to have a look at the glorious view over Garthdale. Climbing steadily she felt she was making very good progress, and the top was not too far away when the path suddenly gave her the choice of two directions. The main path went on to the left, but a narrow rougher path diverged to the right and seemed to lead straight up to the point where she knew the stones must be. The first hundred yards levelled out and she found the walking quite easy, then as the top of the moor loomed over her, the heather got thicker and obscured the path, and she found herself stumbling and falling. Knowing that the top was not too far away, she was not to be beaten, and persevered until the heather thinned out and the last short distance was over stony scree which was not too difficult. At last she was on the top and was overjoyed to find she had judged the direction well and that her pile of stones was only fifty yards away to the east. Her discovery gave her an impetus, and she almost ran those last few yards across the soft turf of the top to get to the stones, sinking on to them thankfully, half-laughing, half-crying. It had taken nearly an hour to reach the top and she knew she mustn't stop too long, even though going down would be so much quicker. It was still light and fine, though she fancied that the cloud hanging over the moor on the opposite side of the dale looked thicker and lower. She hoped it wasn't going to rain, she might be glad of her raincoat yet.

She was usually so relaxed and happy at this point, high above the dale, that it was a hard thing to bring to the forefront of her mind her reasons for being there on this particular evening. The scene in Mark's room seemed remote and unreal, the horror of it was so great that she had a job to convince herself that it had really happened. Could she have spoken to Mark like that? She knew that under extreme provocation her usually equable temper could break and flare up, and in the past under similar circumstances she had often said words that she had afterwards regretted. But regret was not the uppermost of her feelings now, the enormity of the whole affair was that Mark could possibly have seriously considered sending Emma away to school. She knew from the time of Emma's illness that he felt some degree of affection for his daughter, and it was painful to her that he valued Maxine's opinion so much that he had even agreed to think about boarding-school. Helen had no doubt in her mind that Maxine was the prime mover in the whole episode, she refused to believe that Mark was so lacking in feeling for Emma that he would consider sending her away. The thought of the child being sent away from the little security she had in her life, into an unknown, hostile environment, brought a dull sense of sickness; with the sickness was also a sense of shame. She who loved Emma and would do anything to protect her had done the very worst thing she could have done towards helping the little girl. She had shouted, in her rage, unforgiveable things to Mark, and once again tears came to her eyes as she remembered her words and his astonishment. Surely he would never, ever let her stay on after such an outburst, and in a fit of sobbing, burying her face in her hands, the realisation came to her that she had probably not only lost Emma but Mark as well through her own folly.

How long she stayed like that she did not know, as her thoughts sent her heart sinking to the depths, and try as she would she could think of no way out of the tangle she had made by her own outspokenness. As she slowly shook and lifted her head she suddenly felt a moisture that was not tears on the outside of her hands. She looked around her in disbelief. A soft fine rain had come down more like a mist, and all she could see was the stone she sat on. The valley had disappeared as though it had never been there and she got up in a blind panic. She had heard Mrs Rose talk about the cloud coming down on the moor and she remembered the times when it had been clear in Hexton, but she had looked up to the top of the moor to see it shrouded in low cloud. She knew she must be in such a cloud now; it took a lot of resolution and willpower not to take fright and run, but to stay where she was and decide what sensible course of action to take. She thankfully put on her mac, as the low cloud had brought a drop in temperature and putting her hand in her pocket she was glad to find a woollen headscarf and some gloves, stuffed in the last time she had worn it. She carefully made a plan. She knew exactly where she was and how far she had walked along to the stones. If she took the same number of paces back and then struck off downwards she could not fail to come to the fields, and once she got to the fields she was sure she would be out of the cloud. It was usually only the top of the moor that lay covered. She was certain she would not go wrong as long as she kept going down all the time, and she set off straight away with a confidence which was to be short lived. Her inexperience had not taught her that mist is a deceiver. Helen thought she was going straight along the top path, but she suddenly found herself in deep heather and had to edge herself slowly back until she found the path again. She decided it would be better if she started downwards immediately, hoping that in a few minutes she would be free of the cold, damp, clinging mist. She had forgotten the scree she had carefully picked her way round on the way up; now the stones were obstacles, halting her at every step until she found herself almost crawling on hands and knees to get over the low rocks. Still she tried not to panic, just keep going she kept saying to herself, it can't be far now, and when she reached the heather she felt an enormous relief that her plan was working and that she was making some progress. Relief and confidence soon ebbed, as she tripped and fell over the strong tufts, and it didn't seem to come to an end as she thought it should have done. She was almost gasping with despair by now, utterly lost. Soon it would be getting dark, and the cloud showed no sign of thinning. She was brought up short by a low wall and for a moment she thought she had reached the meadows; she followed the wall along, and coming to an opening, discovered that she had made almost a complete circle. Enlightenment came as she remembered seeing the small, stone, circular shooting butts elsewhere on the moor; built like a round stone wall to hide the sportsmen, in the centre they were soft and grassy. She found the entrance and thankfully sank down onto the turf, leaning against the low wall. She breathed hard and tried to think; she had no idea where she was, she had certainly passed no shooting butts on the way up. Perhaps she had made a mistake in trying to find her way down. Too late she seemed to remember someone telling her that if you get caught in low cloud, you should stay where you are until it clears. She shut her eyes in utter dismay at her foolishness. She could be here till morning, and what would they be thinking at Bridge House? Mark knew she had run out, but no one in the house knew in which direction she had gone. They would have no idea where to look for her. In her exhaustion she must have dozed a little and imagined she was dreaming and that Mark was calling her name. She raised her head and opened her eyes, half-listening for the sound that had been in her dream.

'Helen. Helen.'

She stood up, unable to believe that it really was Mark.

'I'm here. Here.' she screamed in excitement. 'Mark, I'm here in the shooting-butt.'

'Stay where you are, and don't move, but keep calling.' Minutes later a tall figure appeared through the gloom, she ran towards him and was caught in a close, hard embrace.

'You little fool,' he said gruffly into the top of her head. 'You darling little fool. What did you mean by running off like that? You could have been on the moor all night.'

Hardly believing what he was saying to her, she held tight to him. 'How did you find me? I never thought you would find me.'

'Never mind that now. I've got to get you

back to the car. Have a drink of this and then hang on to me and we'll be off. It will be dark soon.' He held out a flask of brandy and although she didn't like the strong, fiery liquid, she was glad of the glow of warmth it sent through her, 'I'm not going to stop to talk to you now. That can come later. You probably don't realise that you are only yards from the track that leads to the Wedderdale road and I've got the Range Rover parked there.'

'But how . . .'

'Shut up, not another word. Hold my hand and I'll have you on the track and we'll climb up to the road in no time. If we go wrong I've got my compass.'

She was glad not to have to talk, it took all her time and energy to follow his long strides along the broad track which seemed very easy to follow even in the mist. When they got to the top, she was amazed to find herself on the road where she usually parked the Mini. The sight of the Range Rover looming out of the mist was very welcome.

Mark opened both doors and he didn't waste words. 'Take off that wet mac, and put this thick woolly of mine on. At least you had the sense to take a coat with you. Then get in. They'll be worrying about us at Bridge House, but there is something that has got to be said before we make our way down.'

Helen suddenly trembled. It was not from cold, for she felt warm in Mark's enormous thick sweater which engulfed her, and she was still glowing from the brandy. Nervousness at his reaction, not only to her angry words but also the trouble she had caused in running off, overcame her. He must have felt her convulsive movement as he laid his hand over hers in a gesture of what seemed to Helen to be almost one of reconciliation, but could she hope for that? She started what she knew was going to be a difficult conversation. 'I'm sorry I lost my temper, I said a lot of things that were unpardonable. It was not my place to criticize you, but I was only thinking of Emma . . .' She faltered and stopped, not knowing what kind of reply to expect. When it came, it took her breath away, as it came in the form of an apology, the last thing she had been expecting.

'Helen, I asked you what you thought and you told me honestly and fearlessly. You told me truths which were very hard for me to swallow; I've been aware that I've not been able to make up to Emma for the loss of her mother. I do love Emma but somehow it's been too difficult to give her the affection she needs; something seems to stop me. As though there was a great obstacle in the way which was the memory of Louise. I'm sorry, I'm not making a very good job of this, but I want you to know that what you said, made me think and see things straight for the first time in years. You don't have to say sorry—I do. And I have to say thank you; Emma will not be sent away to school and from now on I'm going to try and be a much better father to her. Will that make you happier?'

Helen was confounded. 'I thought you would be asking me to leave,' was all that she could say, in her astonishment at Mark's words.

'No, Helen, Emma couldn't do without you,' he said, adding in a quiet voice as he started up the engine: 'and I don't think I can either.'

Nothing more was said, and as they crept through the cloud and made their way from the hill, Mark's last words kept running through Helen's mind and were to haunt her for the rest of the evening, until she went wearily and thankfully to bed.


## CHAPTER SEVEN

Mark was true to his word. In the next few weeks, Helen noticed a great change in his attitude towards Emma and this was to bring some happy moments to them all. It so happened that Maxine was very busy making arrangements for an important exhibition at her small country gallery. Through her contacts in the art world, she had got to know Ben Morland, an established American painter in oils. It was his pictures she had on the walls of her living room. He was on a long visit to Europe and after a lengthy period of negotiations, he had agreed to an exhibition of his works at the Hexton Gallery. Some of his paintings were arriving from American museums and galleries, and Maxine was re-arranging the gallery to house the pictures.

She had taken to calling to see Mark much later in the evening, thus creating an ideal opportunity for Mark to spend time with Emma after tea. Summer was now at its height, and both Emma and Helen were delighted when Mark suggested trips to the coast at weekends. Towards the end of June, Emma got it into her head that what she would like more than anything would be a picnic up on the moor. She mentioned it several times, but Helen was not of the opinion that idea of the three of them going on a picnic would appeal to Mark.

On the last Wednesday of the month, the weather being still warm and fine, Emma seemed determined to seize her opportunity at breakfast-time. Mark's head was buried in the morning paper, but he had to raise it to Emma's persistent questions. 'Daddy, I want to ask you something. It's important.'

Mark smiled at her, prepared for the once a month request that she could have a dog. 'Yes, Emma.'

'Is it your afternoon off?' and hardly waiting for him to nod his head in assent, she went on quickly. 'I want us to go for a picnic on the moor. You and Helen and me. I've never been right up on the moor and I keep asking Helen but she never says yes.'

Mark and Helen's eyes met, and in Mark's there was some amusement.

'Fighting shy of the moor, Helen?'

She gave a confused smile. 'No, it's not that. I just didn't think you would want to give up your half day to go on a picnic.'

Emma was looking at them both. 'Daddy's got plenty of time,' she butted in. 'It's the middle of summer and people don't get colds and things.' They both laughed at her and the little joke seemed to set the seal on the arrangement.

'I suppose I could make up a picnic after lunch, then meet you from school and we could set off straight away. Where would you like to go Emma?' asked Helen. 'Do you want to go up the hill in the car?'

'No, I don't,' was the definite reply. 'I want to go over the bridge, over the meadow, through those fields and up to the moor. I'm a good walker and it won't be too steep for me,' she added hastily. The self-assurance amused Helen and Mark and the thought was mutual that Emma was really growing out of her awkwardness and unhappiness at last.

Mark went off on his visits after a brief early lunch and was back at Bridge House well before the time to meet Emma from school. Helen had a picnic ready packed in rucksacks,

153

she had managed to find a small one for Emma to carry.

Mark went up to get changed and came down looking bronzed and relaxed, in a casual short-sleeved biscuit coloured shirt that suited his dark hair. Emma was soon running up the steps and Helen helped her to change into her denims and a shirt. There was no need for jumpers and waterproofs in this settled spell of fine weather.

They followed the route that Emma had described, leaving the river immediately and crossing the meadow to the first of the snickets in the walled fields. The walls in this part of the dale were all in good repair, the art of dry stone walling not having died out. Most farmers repaired their own walls; one of the jobs done in June, the slackest time for the year for dale farmers and the month when, if ever, they took a holiday.

In the corner of the first field stood a sturdy stone building rather like a barn.

'What is that house for, Daddy?' asked Emma.

'It's not a house; it's called a shippon. Years ago when the weather got bad in the winter, the farmer would get all his cows together and keep them in the shippon and feed them there. Nowadays, the cows are brought into the farms, but if you look round, you'll see that most groups of fields have a shippon.'

'Are there any cows in there now? Can I go

154

and have a look?' Mark smiled at the inquisitive little girl. 'We can go and have a look, but I think that all you will find is a heap of hay and a few owls fast asleep until night-time.'

This last remark made Emma all the more determined to have a look at the shippon, and they made a detour round the field so that she could look in.

'Oh, it's not so dark as I thought it would be,' she exclaimed as they peered in. 'It would be a good place to shelter if it rained.'

Emma had been right when she claimed she was a good walker—she strode out, rucksack on her back, usually ahead of Mark and Helen, who walked side by side in quiet companionship behind her. As they came out onto the moor, they called to Emma to take the track straight ahead. Helen was remembering the last time she had come that way and thought in amazement of the difference in her relationship to Mark and of that unhappy day in contrast to this. Emma had stopped at a grassy spot and had climbed up on to the flat grey stones that lay there. 'This would do for our picnic,' she cried out. 'Let's stop here. I can see right over the dale for miles and miles—look how small the farmhouses are. And you can just see the river, can't you?' She pointed to where there was a glint of silver between the trees that bordered the River Garth. Emma had chosen quite a good place, Helen was able to lay out the sandwiches and crisps, apples and bananas. Mark sat down beside her. 'What, no champagne?' he said jokingly.

'Are we celebrating, or something?' she retorted, and he said quietly so that Emma couldn't hear, 'I think we are celebrating someone becoming a normal happy little girl.'

Helen looked at him warmly. 'She is better isn't she? I am so glad, but I'm afraid you'll have to celebrate with orange juice!'

It was a noisy, merry picnic. The climb had given them keen appetites and Emma munched and chatted her way through the pile of sandwiches and then started on the fruit. Half way through a banana, she suddenly stopped eating and looked keenly at Mark and Helen. 'Wouldn't it be nice if it was always like this?'

Helen wondered what was behind the child's question and hardly knew what to say, but Mark deliberately didn't take her seriously. 'Do you mean you would like to come here and have a picnic every day?'

'No, of course not.' If an eight year old could be scornful, Emma certainly succeeded. 'I mean it would be nice if you and Helen could get married and then I would have a father *and* a mother.'

The bombshell of these words fell into a deep startled silence, Mark recovering first and to Helen's dismay taking her hand, holding it firmly and almost forcing her to raise her eyes to his. She could not read his expression, but there was a look, almost of hope; but there was enquiry also and the query crept into his voice as he asked her: 'Well, Helen, what do you think of that idea?'

The way he had asked the question, gave the lie to his seriousness and she tried to answer in similar vein. 'I always did believe that Emma had a vivid imagination, and now I know,' she said, and a small demon inside her made her continue: 'And I think we've both got different ideas, haven't we?'

The spectre of Maxine spoiled the scene and Helen turned to Emma trying to change the subject, but the little girl seemed to have summed up the situation for herself. 'I know what you're going to say. It's like the dog. We'll think about it. Grown-ups are always the same, they never seem to be able to make up their minds.'

The precocious words succeeded in breaking the awkward silence. No more was said, Helen started packing up and Emma was soon quite happy to be racing down the hill, trying to make her father keep up with her, with Helen following thoughtfully in the rear.

As the three of them were going down the path that crossed the last field, Emma ahead as usual, came running back.

'There's Maxine!' she shouted, pointing in the direction of the bridge. Mark and Helen slowed down for a moment and a look of bewilderment came into Mark's face, as he recognised it was indeed Maxine, and as she walked towards them, they realised that it was a very angry and upset Maxine. Mark hurried towards her and took her arm, then Maxine's words floated clearly across the meadow for Helen to hear.

'Wherever have you been? What on earth have you been doing? I waited and waited and you didn't come and we had to go on without you.' Mark was not enlightened by these words and the frown still furrowed his brow, growing deeper at her way of addressing him. His tone was stiff.

'Maxine, you know very well that Wednesday is my afternoon off. It's most unusual for me to make any arrangements to meet you during the afternoon. You are always at the Gallery.'

'Exactly. The Gallery. Don't you remember, even now, what we were supposed to be doing this afternoon?' was the frosty reply.

Mark was obviously thinking desperately in what way he could have let Maxine down, but she gave him no chance to search his memory.

'You had completely forgotten that it was the opening of my Exhibition this afternoon, hadn't you?' It was not horror that dawned on Mark's face; inwardly he could see a trivial and funny side, but dare not show any light-heartedness about his mistake, knowing how important it was to Maxine. She continued in a high-pitched, angry, aggrieved voice. 'A fine fool you made me look, there we were waiting for the local doctor to open the Exhibition, because it is an important local occasion for Hexton, and where was Dr Mark Sinclair? Enjoying himself with his daughter and his receptionist, having a picnic on the moor of all things.'

Mark tried to say something but the flow of wrath was not to be interrupted.

'Ben Morland himself was there, and all the owners of galleries in Leeds, besides a lot of local artists. It's a good job that Ben is an understanding kind of person, he himself had to make the opening speech that you should have made.'

Mark at last got a word in and tried to be calm and gentle with the irate woman. 'Maxine, I'm sorry. What else can I say? You know that I was reluctant to open the Exhibition in the first place. I felt it should have been someone from your art world who knows something about these things.' He added lamely, 'Emma was so keen and excited about having a picnic on the moor, I'm afraid the Exhibition went right out of my mind. What can I do for my appalling forgetfulness? Presumably everyone is still at the Gallery, shall I came back with you now and talk to them?'

She was barely mollified. 'I left them having

a drink, and Ben was showing the press round. I had to go to Bridge House to ask Mrs Rose where you were. Fortunately she knew what your plans were and I found you straight away, so I've not been missing from the Gallery for very long.'

Then she looked at them, taking in the trio of casually dressed people who had just come off the moor. 'You'll have to be quick to change, you can't go like that.'

Mark turned to Helen and gave her his rucksack, their eyes met and Helen's must have shown a degree of sympathy because Mark shrugged and said. 'I'll go and change and hurry on with Maxine, if you will bring Emma back with the rucksacks.' His parting shot, Helen thought, was a dig at Maxine. 'Sorry to break up the happy party.'

The pair hurried off, leaving Helen and Emma to walk slowly home, and Emma couldn't be expected to stay quiet for long.

'Maxine's very angry, isn't she? Sometimes she gets cross with me, even if I haven't been naughty.' Helen looked down at the child, who sometimes seemed older than her years.

'The new Exhibition is very important to Maxine, Emma. And Daddy did break his promise.'

Emma had the last word as they reached Bridge House. 'I suppose that thinking about a dog is not a promise, is it?'

Helen smiled, but said nothing, inwardly

thinking how complex was the child mind, one moment coming out with truths almost of an adult; yet in the same breath, clinging to a childish desire which would not be relinquished.

They unpacked the rucksacks, and after her energetic racing up and down the moor, Emma was satisfied with a quiet hour before she went to bed and fell fast asleep.

Helen was glad to be alone with her thoughts, and as the sun got lower in the sky, she sat out in the shady garden. She tried to put Emma's words out of her mind; the child would obviously like to see the two people she loved best in the world united. But marriage with Mark? She had never given it a thought, knowing and believing him to be Maxine's property; the idea of Mark and Maxine brought a frown, when she thought of Emma, who must be the biggest obstacle between them. Maxine had no time for Emma, and Mark had become much closer to his small daughter in the last four weeks. How could there be a possibility of reconciling the two?

'Why are you sitting frowning like that?' Mark's words were a statement rather than a question, and his silent approach had made her jump at his sudden nearness.

'Oh, Mark,' she cried. 'Was it all right about the Exhibition? I feel guilty taking you off on a picnic like that.'

'Stop feeling guilty, it wasn't your fault, it

was mine; and you didn't take me off, Emma did.'

She gave a quick smile and asked her question again. 'And the Exhibition? I'm afraid Maxine was very angry.'

'Maxine soon got over it. I think it was a fit of personal pique because I didn't turn up. The Exhibition's a great success—this Ben Morland is a showman, he enjoyed opening his own exhibition. Couldn't have cared less that the country doctor wasn't there, though I must say that he's a nice chap. Not the sort to be annoyed at anything like that and seems to know how to handle Maxine when she gets on her high horse. I left them all drinking and looking at those ghastly pictures.' He stopped and their eyes met and they burst out laughing.

'Are they really ghastly?' Helen asked, surprised at Mark's confidentiality. It was not like him to say anything about Maxine.

'Well, I don't like them. You go and see them, and take Emma with you. I'd be interested to know what she thought of them—they looked as though they'd been painted by a child.'

Again Helen laughed, it was the usual comment about contemporary painting by someone who was not an art lover. Mark suddenly bent towards the seat where she was sitting and pulled her to her feet. 'Come for a walk by the river. It's been quite a day and I feel like a gentle stroll by the water. Nice and relaxing.'

He was in an odd kind of mood, Helen thought, as they crossed the bridge and went through the stile to the river path. It was so familiar to her now, and the scene of many encounters, but she never tired of it. Mark took her hand casually and she did not take hers away, nor was she surprised when he said: 'Let's sit by the water for a while.'

She chose to joke and not let the conversation get too serious. 'There's not much water to watch.' It was true; after the fine spell, the river was very low and it would have been possible to have crossed over to the other side if one used the stepping stones carefully.

'Then I'll watch you instead.'

Helen's eyes flew to Mark's face. He was watching her intently and under his penetrating gaze, she let her eyes drop and felt her breath coming faster. At his next words, her breath was completely taken away.

'Helen, will you marry me?'

He was still looking at her, but did not touch her. Her astonishment was so great, that she felt the blood rush to her head and the ensuing confusion of thoughts left her incapable of speech.

'Helen, don't answer for a minute, but listen to me. I know how much you love Emma. You were right when you lost your temper with me; she does need love and since you have found that you have been able to give it to her, she has been a different child. Don't think that she put the idea into my head this afternoon, I've been thinking about it for a long time. You and I get on quite well, sometimes we get on very well, and she does need a mother so badly.' He stopped, still looking at her, then as she remained silent, he took her hand and said gently 'Please think about it; you will, won't you? You don't have to reply now.'

Helen could only think of one word. 'Maxine ...?'

His expression changed and there was a hardness in his features. 'Forget Maxine,' he said tersely.

'But I thought ...' she didn't seem to be able to finish her sentences.

'Never mind what you thought. We'll forget Maxine.'

In her turmoil of emotion, she was unable to look at him. He was asking her to marry him, to forget Maxine, yet he had offered her no word of love, not even of affection. Did he mean a wife in name only, so that Emma would have a mother? He had given no clue to how he felt, and it was not something she could ask. How could she marry without love? She knew that she couldn't.

Mark's voice broke into her thoughts as she struggled to give him a reply.

'Is it Neil, Helen?'

Her eyes flew to his; this was a way of

getting out of a difficult situation, to let him believe that she was still considering Neil's proposal—which was in fact far from the truth.

Falteringly she said, 'I haven't made up my mind yet.'

Stony-faced, he got up and started walking back along the river path, not a word being said between them, even when they parted in the hall at Bridge House. She ran up to her room and flung herself on the bed, bursting into a flood of tears.

She did not know if she was crying for herself, for Mark or for Emma. What she did know, suddenly, forcibly and irrevocably was that what she had just refused, was the one thing she wanted more than anything she had ever wanted in her life.

## CHAPTER EIGHT

The tension was to continue between them the whole of the next day and it was not until Helen went to meet Emma from school, that events were to start to overtake her.

Emma came across the playground, followed closely by Jane, and in Jane's face, Helen could see a look of subdued happiness and excitement. Intuition made her question to Jane come almost unbidden. 'Jane, has Neil . . . ?'

Jane looked at her friend as though she was afraid to say her next words. 'Oh, Helen, Neil has asked me to marry him, I'm so happy. But what about you? I always thought . . .' She was stopped from speaking by Helen, who gave her a big hug. 'It's the nicest news I've heard for a long time, and what I've always hoped for. Neil was a good friend to me Jane, but nothing more. I wish you both every happiness.' She suddenly remembered Emma, and looked down to find her taking in every word, her eyes bright with excitement. 'Is there going to be a wedding?'

Both Helen and Jane laughed as they told her the news, and then Emma reminded Helen that they were supposed to be going to see Maxine's Exhibition. Helen promised to see Jane later in the week and went off with Emma to the Gallery, gladness in her heart and, for once, the thought of Mark far from her mind.

They arrived at the Gallery and as it was almost closing time, there were very few people about. Emma would have much preferred to have looked at the pottery animals, but Helen had explained to her about Ben Morland, and they went up the steps from the shop into the large exhibition room.

Helen's heart sank when she saw the pictures. She knew of Ben Morland's reputation, which was international, but here before her were thirty or forty pictures, modern abstracts of the kind she most disliked. Brilliantly executed and with vibrant colours, the pictures had no appeal for her and she wondered what her small charge was thinking. Then she caught sight of Emma's face; her expression was one of total perplexity.

'Helen,' she said, very loudly, 'I don't like them, they don't make sense, they are just ...' she paused, as though searching for the right word, ' ... splashes.'

Oh dear, thought Helen, and to think I imagined that through a child's eyes the pictures would come alive with meaning; but Emma had already seen enough of the paintings and suddenly hopped down the two steps into the shop and ran full tilt into a figure who was coming through to the Exhibition. It was Mark, and Helen froze when she remembered her last encounter with him; but he chose to ignore her.

'Daddy, have you seen the pictures?'

'I saw them yesterday, Emma, I've just popped in to see Maxine. What do you think of them? They are very clever, aren't they?' Mark wasn't sure if he had used the right word and as his eyes met Helen's, he gave her an unexpected grin and she knew that they shared the same opinion about the masterpieces.

'I think,' declared Emma, as though she had considered it very carefully, 'that the paintings are nice and bright, but not clever.'

'You look and see if you can find one you really like and perhaps we'll buy it,' replied Mark and went off into Maxine's office.

Emma tugged at Helen's hand. 'Helen,' she said 'There's a picture I would like but it's not here. It's in the shop. Come and look. I've seen it before.'

They went into the shop and Emma pointed to the picture just at the foot of the steps. Helen couldn't help smiling; all her own and the child's love of the dales was embodied in that picture. It was by a local artist and all you could call it was a field full of sheep; but in it, the painter had captured all the atmosphere and colour of the dale, the greys and greens, the whites and the feeling of space and solitude, quietness and permanence. They stood looking at it together and before Helen had a chance to make a comment, raised voices could be heard from Maxine's office. In all the time she had known Mark she had heard his voice raised in anger only twice, and now he sounded very, very angry. Rooted to the spot, his voice pierced her consciousness and she forgot everything: Emma, where she was, everything except what Mark was saying.

'Maxine, will you please listen to what I have to say to you . . .'

But a high-pitched wheedling voice interrupted him. 'Oh, Mark. Don't be so hasty. We have never quarrelled. It wouldn't be a problem that Emma doesn't like me. If she was

168

sent away to school . . .'

'Maxine!' Mark exploded. 'I've told you never to mention school again. As far as Emma is concerned, her place is with me. You say we've never quarrelled, well, we're quarrelling now. We've had a good time in the past, but it's over. Do you hear? Over. You'd better get together with your artist friend Ben Morland. I'm sure that he would have far more patience with you than I have, and you would fit much more happily into their little worlds . . .'

Still the angry voice went on, when Helen came to her senses and thought of Emma. She looked round; the child had disappeared from her side. She glanced round the now empty gallery and hunted round the shop. There was no sign of her. Emma had gone. Frantically Helen rushed into the road outside the Gallery; it was deserted; in one direction it led through a group of cottages to the river, the opposite way went straight into the square. Helen thought that the most likely thing that Emma would have done was to have run home, it was obvious that her disappearance from the Gallery must have been the result of hearing Maxine say that she would be sent away to school, something which had always terrified her. She had gone before she had time to hear the answer that her father had so forcibly given to Maxine's suggestion.

Now in the square, almost empty of late

afternoon shoppers, Helen looked wildly round, but there was no sign of Emma. 'She must be at home,' said Helen to herself firmly, as she hurried into Bridge Street.

In the kitchen at Bridge House, she found Mrs Rose preparing the tea. Helen's words came with a rush. 'Mrs Rose, Emma has run away. Have you seen her? She was with me in the Gallery and she accidentally heard something that Maxine said about her being sent away to school. I can't find her anywhere.' She looked imploringly at the housekeeper as though Mrs Rose might be able to conjure Emma up from somewhere behind the kitchen table. Mrs Rose, with calm commonsense helped Helen to search the house, and then they went into the garden, though by this time it was becoming obvious that Emma had not come home.

'What shall we do?' frowned the worried Helen. 'I wish Mark was here. I suppose he is still at that wretched gallery.'

Helen was wrong. After his furious quarrel with Maxine, Mark had stormed out of the Gallery, and as he turned into the square he literally bumped into Neil and Jane. Apologising for his haste, he suddenly realised that he was looking into a pair of radiantly happy and smiling faces. Forgetting his recent flare up with Maxine, he had a sudden happy conviction and asked them straight out. 'Hey, you two! Have you got some news to tell me?'

Neil knew Mark the better of the two and he held out his hand to the doctor. 'It's congratulations, Mark. Jane has said she will marry me. You are about the first to know as it's only just happened. We are just off to Jane's flat and I am going to try and persuade her to make it a summer wedding.'

Mark grinned his pleased congratulations. 'I couldn't be more happy and you have lifted a weight from my shoulders. Jane won't mind me saying that for a time I thought it was Helen who was going to be the lucky girl.'

Neil gave him a knowing glance. 'Helen is a lovely girl, but I never stood a chance. There was always someone else.'

'Was there indeed?' Understanding was clear in Mark's face. 'Look, you two, I must run and catch Helen up straight away.'

As Mark went up the steps of Bridge House, Helen came running down and hurled herself at him. He gripped her arms. 'Just the person I want to see, you let me think you were going to marry Neil . . .'

'Mark, listen to me, it's Emma.' She tried to interrupt him, but he had only one thought in mind.

'Never mind about Emma, and trying to change the subject. I've just met Jane and Neil and they tell me they are getting married. Neil and Jane, do you hear?'

'Mark, will you listen, Emma has run away.' Helen was shouting in her effort to get Mark's attention, but still he took no notice, and pulling her close, his voice drowned her objections. 'I don't want to hear about Emma, I want to hear about you, and you are going to tell me, now.' He stopped as she burst into tears and struck out at him.

'I hate you, let me go, I must go and look for Emma, you never have cared for her ...' She broke off as he seemed to realise at last the extent of her upset behaviour. Speaking more calmly but not letting her go, he looked into her face. 'Helen, what are you saying? You'd better calm down and tell me.'

She sobbed into his chest. 'Emma is missing. She's nowhere. We can't find her; she heard what Maxine said about being sent away to school and she ran off and I didn't even notice. I was listening ...' she halted, realising that she was confessing to the fact that she had eavesdropped on their quarrel. Mark, still holding her close to him, was grim faced. 'Go on,' he said.

'I was listening to you and Maxine quarrelling and I didn't even see Emma go. I'm sorry, I'm sorry. What shall we do?'

He put his arm round her shoulders and coaxed her up the steps into the house. A distressed Mrs Rose, repeated Helen's words. 'Oh, doctor, I'm glad you've come. What shall we do?'

Mark looked seriously from one to another. 'We will all sit down and Mrs Rose will make some tea quickly, and while we are drinking it, you will tell me exactly where you have looked already.'

He listened grimly to Helen's story. 'You have checked all the places here and near to home, and now we will have to think further afield. Emma has had a shock and her first instinct was to run away from us, but you must remember that she is only small, and I have a strong feeling that she is not far away, if only we knew where to look. Now let's put our heads together and think of the most likely spots. Places where she has hidden before, or places she likes to go to.'

'We could try the school,' suggested Helen.

'Good idea.' agreed Mark. 'Better still, we will get Jane and Neil to check the school. You go and phone them and tell them what has happened. They are at Jane's flat.'

Helen rushed to the phone, and Mrs Rose and Mark tried to think of all the likely places that Emma might have run to. When Helen came back, he took her hand and squeezed it. 'Is it OK?'

'Yes, they will go round to the school, and search the field and the hedge where she used to hide. Have you had any ideas?'

'You tell me this. Where would you say that Emma's favourite places are?'

Helen considered. 'She likes walking along the river, she likes going to the Kirkby's farm but she couldn't get there.' She suddenly brightened 'She loved going up on the moor when we had the picnic. Do you suppose she could have climbed all the way up there?'

Mark took her hands. 'Let's go and look,' he said, and smiled his encouragement.

Glad to have something to do, Helen followed Mark quickly down the road to the bridge. She took his hand as they walked along the river path, her eyes constantly straying up to the moor. 'Mark, she's not here, let's go to the rocks where we had the picnic.'

He looked down at her and said slowly: 'Perhaps you're right. Cheer up, sweetheart, she can't have gone far in this short time. Come on, the sooner we get to the top, the better.'

Helen looked at him doubtfully. 'I wish I felt as hopeful as you. Poor little Emma, she has been so happy lately.'

'And she will be again,' was the reply as he strode off across the meadow. Helen had a job to keep up with him as they crossed the fields and paused to get her breath. As she stood, she realised she was looking at the stone barn in the corner of the field. A stirring within her made her call out. 'Mark, Mark, wait. The shippon. She may be hiding there. I'm going to have a look.' Before he had time to turn back to her, she was racing across the field as though she couldn't reach the small building quickly enough. She slowed down as she got there for fear her hopes would be dashed. But as she stood in the opening of the stone wall that served for an entrance, she could hardly stop herself shouting for joy. There, lying fast asleep on a pile of hay, was Emma. Helen crept closer and bent over her, noticing the tear-stained face and her crumpled school dress. She sank down by Emma's side and buried her face in her hands, the tears flowed freely in the release of worry and tension. Then she felt a hand on her shoulder and looked up to meet the eyes of a smiling Mark as he held out his arms to her. As he held her close he whispered into her hair. 'Let her sleep. I've got a lot to say to you, the most important being that I love you.'

Helen looked into his eyes and words were forgotten, his lips claimed hers in a kiss of such depth and passion that she felt the fiery merging of his body to hers. She arched herself closer to him, her arms round the back of his neck, her fingers threading through the short dark hair. She gasped as she felt his hand trace the line of her back through her thin cotton dress; torrents of fire threatened to engulf her as he found her tender young breast. His lips left hers and found the soft flesh above her breast, that his hand was so sensuously caressing. Her own lips, now muffled in his neck, tried to utter words of sense, that did not want to come. 'Mark, Mark,' she murmured, over and over again, and tried to draw herself away. 'We must think of Emma.'

Something of what she said must have penetrated his consciousness, for he suddenly used both his arms to enfold her in an embrace which held warmth and comfort, love and desire, telling her once and for all that this was what he wanted, and she knew it was where she wanted to be. His kisses now were gentle, touching the top of her head, the side of her mouth. He whispered softly. 'I know that this is not the time or the place . . .' His words were interrupted by a sleepy eager voice. 'Daddy, why are you kissing Helen?'

They jumped apart and faced the small figure on the hay. She was looking at them with great big enquiring eyes, waiting for an answer. It came from Mark. 'I'm kissing Helen because I love her.'

'I love her too.'

But Mark was remembering why they were there, and knew he had to take his small daughter to task. 'If you love Helen, why did you run away? You have made Helen, and all of us very unhappy. We didn't know where to look for you.'

Emma jumped up and hugged Helen round the legs and Helen picked her up and handed her over to Mark. Emma buried her face in his shoulder and they just managed to hear her words. 'I heard Maxine tell you I would have to go away to school, and I won't, and if you marry Maxine, I shall run away again.'

'I don't want to hear anything about running

away. I am not going to marry Maxine—ever.'

Emma jumped out of his arms and turned to Helen and said emphatically, 'That's good. You can marry him now.'

Mark and Helen's eyes met, not a word was spoken, but the meaning was clear. Helen felt shy and to cover her confusion turned to Emma. 'You have caused enough trouble for one day, but we have found you and now we must take you home as everyone else is very worried about you.'

They all hurried down across the meadow towards the river, through the stile and on to the bridge where they were surprised to find Maxine and Ben Morland coming toward them. Emma shrank against Helen, but Maxine's voice was pleasant and seemed to reassure her. She spoke to Mark. 'I'm sorry, Mark, we heard that Emma was missing and I think it must have been my fault.' Then she smiled across at Ben and the good-hearted American put his arm around her. 'Ben has been talking to me, and I am going to sell the gallery and go back to America with him.'

Mark shook hands with Ben and touched Maxine on the arm. 'I am very pleased and hope that you will find much happiness together.' Ben's broad smile told how much he appreciated Mark's words and they all walked back to Bridge House together, where they said their farewells.

Inside the big, old friendly house, they

found Neil and Jane and Mrs Rose anxiously waiting in the kitchen. There were hugs and tears and explanations and Mrs Rose insisted that they all sat down to tea. When the meal was finished, Mark touched Helen lightly on the arm. 'We'll leave them to the washing up, come down to the river, I've got something to say to you.' They slipped unnoticed out of the front door, and were soon on the river path Mark was silent, his arm held loosely round Helen's waist, and they walked, slowly, lingeringly in the bright evening sunshine. Helen was also quiet; she knew that Mark would speak when he was ready and she was in no hurry. From time to time she felt his lips touch the top of her head, but she did not look up. In the shade of the trees, Mark turned her to face him, his finger touched her chin and tilted her face towards him so that he could look deep into her eyes; looking for the message that he was sure he would find written there. Her clear expression shone with an emotion that could only be love, and he bent down and kissed her softly on the lips. There was no passion in the kiss, and that was not his mood; she felt gentleness and firmness, the knowledge that this was what he wanted; she knew now, at last, that her love was returned

He leaned his cheek against hers and quietly said. 'Helen, my darling, you know that I love you. Can you believe that I have never felt like this before. It is no use hiding what was in the past, you know it all, but what I felt for Louise cannot be compared to what I have come to feel for you. I'm sorry that there is a past, do you think that we can put it behind us and build a future between us?'

Helen looked at him gently and put a finger on his lips. 'You don't have to say it. I understand and don't forget that if there hadn't been a Louise, there wouldn't have been Emma, and if there hadn't been Emma, there might not have been . . . us.'

He hugged her to him. 'You really do understand; I don't deserve it.'

'You don't deserve what?'

'I don't deserve to be loved by someone as wonderful as you.'

She laughed in reply to this statement, her eyes dancing. 'And who told you that I loved you?'

He looked at her, saw that she was not serious, crushed her to him, and his kiss showed her what love meant. A kiss no longer gentle, but teasing, opening her lips which parted so readily, as she gave herself to him without thought of restraint; wholeheartedly showing him her love and her longing for him.

He raised his head and kissed her closed lids. 'Now tell me that you don't love me.'

The eyes opened and he knew that he could read her love, but he wanted to hear the sweet words.

'Helen?'

'I love you, Mark. I can hardly remember a time when I didn't love you.'

'And yet you said no, when I asked you to marry me?' His words were a question which she was ready to answer.

'I knew I loved you then, Mark, but all you asked me was if I would look after Emma. You didn't say that you loved me and I couldn't contemplate a marriage in name only. That's why I let you go on thinking that Neil was still in my thoughts, even though I knew I would never marry him.'

He twisted her long hair in his fingers and held her hand close in his. 'I was a fool; we've got a lot of things to think about. Do I need to ask you, if you will marry me soon. I need you so badly and Emma does too.'

Helen smiled. 'I can't wait.'

'There is one thing I would like to ask, Helen. I know it's traditional for the bride to be married in her home town, but do you think you would mind if we got married in Hexton?'

Helen had no hesitation. 'I want to get married in Hexton, I know so many people here, and I have a deep sense of belonging. I haven't lived at home for several years and I'm sure my family would love to come here.'

He gave a sigh of relief. 'I hoped you would say that. You love the dale, don't you, Helen? Just like I do. You don't yearn for the city lights like Louise and Maxine.'

She shook her head. 'There's nowhere else I

want to be; I feel at home here.'

They both looked at the top of the moor, then at the river, getting narrower and narrower until it started as a small stream at the dale head. The patchwork of fields and limestone walls, so orderly; the greys and greens, all part of the eternal landscape. Each farm they could see, each cottage, they knew housed people who were their people. Helen voiced both their thoughts. 'It's ours,' she said solemnly and as he stroked her soft hair, he laid his face on her forehead and whispered. 'I used to think it was all mine, and now we can truly say those wonderful words "It's ours." I never thought I would find anyone who would share my feelings and think about the dale in the same way as I did. It won't be an exciting life, Helen, but it will be a satisfying one.'

He pulled her to him and passion flared up between them once again. At the end of a lingering kiss, into which both of them poured all their longing and their love, Helen lifted her head and looked at him and said shyly. 'Mark, won't it be lovely to have a family of our own?'

He looked at the slight flush on her cheeks, the sparkling clear quality of her eyes, and when he spoke, his words left her in no doubt of their meaning. 'Darling Helen, you are so beautiful and desirable, I think I will carry you right back to Bridge House and we'll start a family straight away.'

At her adorable confusion, he crushed her to him, but this time it was a quick kiss and a sensible remark. 'That reminds me that there are several people at Bridge House who will be wondering where we have been all this time, though I don't doubt that they will have guessed what we've been up to!'

Home once again, they found Emma in the garden; she raced up to them and then stopped. 'Oh,' she said, wonderingly, 'are you . . . 'She stopped, stuck for words.

Mark bent towards her and took her hands. 'Helen is going to marry me,' he said gently and waited for the response.

When it came it was explosive. 'They're going to get married; they're going to get married!' She danced round in a circle. 'Helen and Daddy are going to get married.' She flung her arms round Helen's neck. 'Does it mean you will never go away?'

Helen kissed the small child she had come to love as her own. 'I will never go away, Emma. Are you pleased?' There was no need for an answer, it was written in Emma's happy face.

'I must go and tell Mrs Rose that we're having a wedding.' She ran off, but suddenly stopped and rushed back to them. 'Oh, and just one more thing, if you are going to get married, do you think, does it mean that I could have a little dog?' she looked at them both, beseeching them not to say the words she always dreaded. But she need not have worried, there were no ifs and buts, and the answer came in a chorus. 'Yes, Emma.' And without a word she gave a joyous leap and ran into the house, leaving Mark and Helen to stroll to the end of the garden. Putting his hands on her shoulders, Mark looked at her with a delighted expression. 'No problems there,' he said. 'My darling, you've worked miracles in this house and you've worked a miracle for me too. It's a wonderful moment. Is it wonderful for you too, Helen?'

Her lips gave him his reply, the soft, gentle pressure telling him of a love that would be undying and as she returned the kiss, Helen knew that his love would be an endless delight, filling her body, her heart and her mind for the rest of her life.